Sarah's
GROUND

Also available by ANN RINALDI

Taking Liberty

Sarah's GROUND

ANN RINALDI

Simon Pulse
New York London Toronto Sydney

SIMON PULSE
An imprint of Simon & Schuster Children's Publishing Division
1230 Avenue of the Americas, New York, NY 10020
Text copyright © 2004 by Ann Rinaldi
All rights reserved, including the right of reproduction
in whole or in part in any form.
SIMON PULSE and colophon are registered trademarks of
Simon & Schuster, Inc.
Also available in a Simon & Schuster Books for Young Readers
hardcover edition.
The text of this book was set in New Caledonia.
Manufactured in the United States of America
First Simon Pulse edition August 2005
10 9 8 7 6 5 4 3 2 1
The Library of Congress has cataloged the hardcover edition as follows:
Rinaldi, Ann.
Sarah's ground / Ann Rinaldi.—1st ed.
p. cm.
Summary: In 1861, eighteen-year-old Sarah Tracy, from New York state, comes to work at Mount Vernon, the historic Virginia home of George Washington, where she tries to protect the safety and neutrality of the site during the Civil War, and where she encounters her future husband, Upton Herbert.
Includes historical notes.
ISBN 0-689-85924-4 (hc.)
1. Mount Vernon (Va. : Estate)—Juvenile fiction. 2. Tracy, Sarah—Juvenile fiction. 3. Herbert, Upton—Juvenile fiction. 4. United States—History—Civil War, 1861–1865—Juvenile fiction. [1. Mount Vernon (Va. : Estate)—Fiction. 2. Tracy, Sarah—Fiction. 3. Herbert, Upton—Fiction. 4. United States—History—Civil War, 1861–1865—Fiction. 5. Diaries—Fiction.] I. Title.
PZ7.R459 Sar 2004
[Fic]—dc22   2003018334
ISBN 0-689-85925-2 (pbk.)

*To Gina and Roger, who will always
have wit and wisdom*

Sarah's
GROUND

One

My older sister, Fanny, put me in a closet once when we were children. She, being the elder, had her reasons, I suppose. I can think of half a dozen reasons right now why she may have done it. I was always a plague to Fanny. Like the time I stole her pearl hair comb when she was going to a party where Herman Melville was to be guest of honor. Mr. Melville came from Troy, New York, where I come from.

We have both a small farm and a town house in Troy, across from the Hart-Cluett mansion. Life there was not dull. But it was confining. Before I made the decision to come to Washington City, my life was like I was in a closet.

Always I was watched. Always I was under someone else's supervision. If it wasn't Fanny's, it was that of one of my older brothers or sisters-in-law, who were, in their own words, "taking the problem away from my parents."

Or it was the teachers at Troy Female Seminary. That was on Mount Ida, above the city, where in the rarified air I learned how to stand straight, play the pianoforte, and stitch a fine seam, to say nothing of science, mathematics, French and philosophy, deportment and dancing.

Always I failed deportment.

"Face your problems head-on, girls. Stare them in the eye," Miss Semple used to say. She was the headmistress, and when she was not telling us to face our problems, she was telling us to express our opinions, but never to be pushy. Pushy girls were the worst sinners in her book. They were to be abhorred. She would not tolerate pushy girls at Troy Female Seminary.

She never explained to us how we were supposed to face our problems head-on without being pushy. I supposed it was a secret we would all learn someday.

Oh, how often I wanted to run away! If it had been sixty years earlier, I might have dressed like a man and run for a pirate ship. In George Washington's time I'd have donned breeches and a rifle frock, taken up a musket, and joined a regiment to fight the British. Or gone west, over the Shenandoahs, to face the Indians. Where indeed I would have been pushy.

But somehow I finished Troy Female Seminary, if only to keep from breaking my parents' hearts. They are considerably older than most parents are with a daughter my age. And being so, it is to be expected that their hearts are very fragile. I was reminded of that constantly by my older brothers, George and Albert.

All my life I have done what my family wanted. I have performed and made them happy. Until now. Now I have broken out on my own. I have applied for a position at Mr.

Washington's home as a sort of live-in caretaker. When I told my parents that it was backed by honorable people, they consented. And I got their friends the Maxwells and the Goodriches, who have money and influence, to write me letters of recommendation.

Oh, I won't exactly be a caretaker. I will have servants and won't have to clean or scrub or even cook. But I will be making decisions about the house, which has long been neglected. Not alone, of course. Miss Cunningham, who is to interview me today, will be there.

And a man called Mr. Upton Herbert. He is the superintendent. At least that's the way it was when I first wrote the letter to Miss Cunningham. But now things have changed.

It is spring of 1861 as I sit here in my room of the Willard Hotel and write this. And South Carolina has seceded from the Union since I wrote that first letter. And war is coming. Things couldn't have changed more than that. But I feel safe here, as if things will turn out well.

Even if Miss Cunningham is from South Carolina. And already she has written to me that she fears she may be needed at home. As if South Carolina has actually broken off from the continent and is about to float out into the Atlantic Ocean.

But she has been honest with me. She has told me that Mount Vernon is in a dilapidated state. That General Washington's great-great-grandnephew, or whatever Mr.

John Augustine Washington is, has left Mount Vernon by now, being the last Washington to have residence there, with all those children of his. Six, I think.

She has told me she is not well, so likely it will be up to me to try to bring to the place some semblance of what it once was.

But that is not what worries me. What worries me is that I have not been honest with her.

And I am afraid she will find me out.

I told her I was twenty-two in my letter. And I am only eighteen, going on nineteen. The Maxwells didn't mention my age in their letter. I know because I read it. Neither did the Goodriches. Not that they were conspiring. They just didn't. And my parents know nothing about the deception. No, the lie is all my own.

So I sit here in my room and worry the matter. But I wouldn't stand a chance at getting the position if I hadn't lied. Oh well, it will all be over soon, and I will either shortly be hired or leave here in disgrace. And, as Miss Semple said, I must face up to the problem.

Within the hour I am to meet with Miss Cunningham.

I sit here writing in my journal. I think I shall try to keep a journal. After all, it isn't every day one gets invited to live in the home of the father of one's country. Something important may happen. And if it doesn't, then I must learn to make important the little things that do happen every day. I must learn that I am important.

If I had learned that a long time ago, I wouldn't be living

like a gypsy, getting shipped place to place by my family. But more about that later.

Here at Willard's I have stayed in my room, fearful of taking to the streets, of even going into the lobby, advised against it by the concierge.

"Congress is in session, miss. The halls, parlors, and dining room are loud and crowded. The din is frightful. We can deliver meals to your room."

They say that to be seen here at Willard's marks one as important. They say they serve fifteen hundred of a Sunday when Congress is in session. But I keep to my room. I don't particularly want to be seen. I want to stay right here, away from it all.

The Federal City is a bedlam. Everybody expects war to happen soon, and the streets are filled with office seekers, soldiers, plug-uglies, hangers-on, and if all that were not bad enough, the elite who have come to see and criticize our backwoods president.

If Miss Cunningham does not approve of me, what shall I do? Go home to Troy to help Father plant the spring corn? Go back to Mount Savage in Maryland to be a governess for the Maxwell children?

I suppose I could stay with my friend Mary McMakin in Philadelphia for a while.

Mayhap if Miss Cunningham doesn't like me, I'll run away to sea.

~

It is terrible being the youngest in the family. I was never spoiled. I was admonished, preached to, and told by my much older siblings that I was the blessing of my parents' old age. And constantly reminded to act like a blessing. But being a blessing can be a tiresome business. My older siblings—George, Albert, and Fanny—raised me for the most part. When home from school, I mostly stayed at one of their houses or the other. Mother's heart really is weak. And Father lost his arm in the Mexican War. Still, he manages to be a gentleman farmer who owns the largest mercantile in Troy. My brothers run it for him. I think my older siblings put this burden of being a blessing on me so I wouldn't be a worry to them, or my parents. And never, never was I taken seriously about anything.

I think that is why I am doing this. To be taken seriously. To have a part in what is going on around me.

Of course, when I applied for this position, my sister, Fanny, didn't help my situation any. She's forever buzzing in my parents' ears about me. "You're going to allow her to be alone? In that place? I hear it's falling down around the superintendent's ears! And do you know who the superintendent is? They say he's the most eligible bachelor in Fairfax County. Mother, you're not going to let her go there!"

Fanny really took on about it. Which I don't understand. Miss Cunningham will be there with me. And for two years, since I graduated from Mrs. Mercier's Academy for

Young Ladies in New Orleans, after I completed Troy Female Seminary, my family has been shipping me about like a Christmas fruitcake to find a husband. And now that I pursue a position where there is a young man present, they are all ready to have me put in a lunatic asylum.

I have not yet met the most eligible bachelor in Fairfax County, but he is safe from me. I must remember to tell him. The last thing I want right now, with war coming, is a husband. There are too many things to be done, not the least of them is to write a book. I really want to do that someday. I intend to do all of the things I want.

But I started to tell how I've been shipped around. And if I'm going to keep a journal about my experience, I must be coherent. It was, of course, to find a husband. After all, what do you do with a young lady recently graduated from two of the nation's best schools, and possibly overeducated to boot? You ship her out.

First there was six months at No. 1 Washington Square with the Grahams, friends of Father's, where I was touted as an excellent dinner companion and conversationalist. Three months with the Maxwells on Savage Mountain in Maryland in the summer—not an official governess, no, but somehow I was always reading to, and looking after, the children. Another six months with the Goodriches in Philadelphia. Mrs. Goodrich is some sort of kin to Mother. And very wealthy.

If I never go to another dinner party in my life, I shall be happy. If I never have to sit through another play in the theater, I shall be ecstatic. As for teas, soirees, hearing professors talk about Robert Burns or Sir Walter Scott, chaperoned walks in the park with insipid young men, I am sick to the teeth of all of it.

"Mrs. Lincoln found her husband that way," Mother told me. "She was visiting her sister in Springfield, Illinois, when they met."

"She was shipped there by her father and stepmother," I said. But I mustn't be saucy to Mother. Brother George would not tolerate it. I sighed. They might as well put a tag on my ear and ship me to Kentucky to a horse auction. Let my husband look for me, is what I say.

Oh dear, I wonder what Miss Cunningham will be like.

I know she wants someone educated, bright, agreeable, and ready with her pen and her tongue. Well, I'm all that. Most times Fanny says I'm too ready with my tongue. I must watch myself. When Miss Cunningham wrote back setting up this appointment, she sounded so befuddled, poor lady, worrying about the war that was warming up on the horizon, worrying about getting home to South Carolina, worrying about her eyes, which give her no end of trouble, and her sister's boy, who was going to join up.

Let's hope, Lord forgive me, that her eyes are not that good, so she won't see my youth. I'm counting on that.

"We need someone of stout purpose and solid values," she wrote.

Heavens! I'm not applying to be secretary to President Lincoln! I told her she had that person. She would soon be looking at her. Though my purpose in life has never been stout, between Troy Female Seminary and the academy in New Orleans I learned enough life values to choke a hungry mule.

What I need is a place to put them to work. I need not to be shuffled around anymore, from family friend to family member, like one of Professor Thaddeus Lowe's balloons. I saw one the other day. Near the White House. Was he demonstrating it? Some people say he is mad, others say he is heaven sent. His wife runs around with a wagon and meets him and helps him cart it off.

As it is, the only man I ever felt an attraction for was Charles Mercier. His mother ran the school in New Orleans. He was quite the most handsome young man I ever met, and if I ever intended to marry, I had decided that I would marry him.

He never talked about Robert Burns or Sir Walter Scott. He didn't like plays. His open, friendly face was always ruddy because he was always outdoors. He wanted to raise horses. He was crazy about his horses.

And he was sent to a military academy because of me.

Because we walked the streets of New Orleans unchaperoned one evening.

There was talk. And talk is the worst thing a proper

young woman from a proper family can afford to let happen to her.

The whole school and all Mrs. Mercier's high-toned friends and the parents of her students were gossiping.

And then it all came out that we'd been sneaking out to meet. And it was then that I decided to leave. To spare her the censure of her high-toned friends. To allow her to keep her students.

Charles and I scarce knew each other, now that I think of it. We hadn't even kissed. All I knew was that he was tall and that his face held all I wanted to know of the world at the time. His eyes were on speaking terms with the stars. His mouth, oh, and how dear and gentle of manner he was, with just enough sadness in him to bring out a girl's mothering instincts. Was it puppy love? I don't know, but I have lived through it, and I don't wish ever to be in love again, thank you. And I shall always remember him as being dear and good.

Oh, it is almost time to go down and meet with Miss Cunningham. I must straighten my hair and look of stout purpose. I must stare my problem in the eye.

Two

I have the job! I have the job!

Miss Cunningham is a dear. A small, nervous lady who wears hoops and a shawl and spectacles, yet still can't see well enough. She desperately needs someone to keep records when she takes over Mount Vernon, to write letters to the Association, and to do other correspondence. I suspect she needs someone to read her mail to her too.

She is just so glad that I come well recommended. Besides the letters from the Maxwells and the Goodriches (who have influence), she had a letter about me from a Mr. Gould (who has means) stating my qualifications. "Lovely to look at," the letter said, "knows French as well as English, dresses with a French influence, schooled in New Orleans." *That can't all be me*, I told myself. And I felt guilty for being an impostor. But then, I suppose most people are, when you get down to it. And I suppose, too, that living with all these high-toned people for the past two years has done something for me after all.

And I discovered that Miss Cunningham herself holds sway over many people.

She is the head of the Association that purchased

Mount Vernon. She is the regent, the high-muck-a-muck, the queen bee. There is a vice-regent in every state, she told me, who is a lady of great esteem. Without getting boring about it, under Miss Cunningham's influence they purchased Mount Vernon from Mr. John Augustine Washington only after ·much persuasion. They paid $200,000!

The place was falling down around everybody's ears, for heaven's sake. Lord knows why Mr. John Augustine neglected it so. Mayhap he didn't have the money, what with six children to support. Imagine that! A Washington not having the money. Isn't life sad sometimes?

Anyway, she knows everybody, this lady. And to raise money she and the Association got Currier and Ives, printmakers, to issue a series of Mount Vernon pictures. They have gotten *Harper's Monthly* magazine to run an illustrated article. And Mr. Godey's *Lady's Book* to endorse the plan to preserve Washington's home and grave, and to solicit subscriptions for donations. Miss Cunningham even knows old Colonel Seaton, who has been running the *National Intelligencer* since 1812.

This is a serious undertaking. Important people are involved. There is nothing frivolous about it, and now I am rather frightened.

Suppose they find out I am only eighteen? Will they think me dishonest? Will they put me in jail? What rule have I broken this time?

Oh, I mustn't think of that. Miss Cunningham says I remind her of her daughter. We had a high tea in Willard's ladies' tearoom. The waitress whispered that a colored woman came to the hotel this morning who is named Elizabeth Keckley. And she is to be a dressmaker for Mrs. Lincoln. She came at the behest of a Miss Whitney from New York, to take that lady's measurements.

Oh, it's exciting being here.

Miss Cunningham asked me what I think of Mr. Lincoln. It was part of the interview. What do I think of him? Why, I hadn't really given him much thought yet, though I think he will be a good man. He seems honest enough, I told her. And humble. And then I gave her the proper answer, the one I knew she wanted to hear.

"I have no feelings one way or the other," I told her. "I have vowed to remain neutral in the coming fray."

She was pleased. *Don't forget,* I told myself, *she is a Southerner.* For the moment, of course, I knew I was violating one of Miss Semple's commandments, which is never to give an opinion just to please somebody. But oh, I did want the job. But right or wrong, I really do not have an opinion of Mr. Lincoln. How could I? He came to us from the wild middle states and nobody knows him. He is a stranger amongst us.

Then she said she had one more question and we would be finished. But I never found out what that question was. Because at that moment there was a commotion in the room. Whisperings, which quickly became an excited buzz.

All started by the waitress. "Oh dear," said one young woman, who let her cup clatter into her saucer. She looked at us and said loudly, "The waitress says Virginia has seceded! Oh, we are from Virginia. We must go home! Where is my husband? Oh, I am in a foreign country!"

And she knocked her teacup off the table in her rush to stand.

I went to help her. She looked about to faint. I succeeded in quieting her. There were tears in her eyes. "I no longer belong here now," she said sadly. "Oh, I have never been to a foreign country!"

When I got back to our table, Miss Cunningham looked at me. "I suppose I don't belong here either," she said. "We will leave first thing tomorrow."

"Tomorrow?" I asked.

"We must shop first. So many things are needed for the house. Why, it doesn't even have kitchen utensils! And we need curtains for the parlor and library. I was thinking red. What do you think, dear?"

"Curtains?" I was starting to sound like the village idiot. Shop? Virginia had just seceded and people would be wild on the streets outside, and this lady wanted to shop for red curtains!

And then I pulled myself together and looked the problem in the eye. Miss Semple would have been proud of me. "Of course," I said, "I think red will be fine."

~

You could see the flowering Judas trees along the riverbanks from the street outside, and because it was spring,
there were vendors selling fresh shad from wagons.
Everywhere you looked there were soldiers and people
scurrying to and fro. Newspaper boys shouted the headlines about Virginia seceding, so the papers must have
printed extra editions. There seemed to be a buzz of
excitement on the street. The militia was drilling in open
spaces. A man in ragged clothes was playing "Listen to the
Mockingbird" on a flute. Everything had about it a sense
of unreality.

I wondered if people would take Miss Cunningham for
a South Carolinian because of her accent. I worried for her.
Then I saw two baggage wagons, piled high with trunks
and boxes, rumbling through the street. "Virginians are
already leaving," Miss Cunningham said. But she was not
worried.

With a hand wearing a white kid glove she hailed a
hack and we got in. She knew where to go. Our trip took
us past the Capitol park, where the horse chestnut blos-
soms gave out a fragrance, where more militia drilled and
regiments of soldiers lounged around on the grass as if no
one had ever heard the word *secession*. Another regiment, whose banner said RHODE ISLAND, was watching a
wedding.

"The *Star* wrote about it," our driver said, slowing down

to get a good look. "Says the bride refused to be left at home and came along with the regiment, so they're getting hitched."

The girl wore a cherry-colored satin blouse, blue pants like the rest of the regiment, and a felt hat turned up on one side with a white plume.

"The world has gone mad," Miss Cunningham said. "Driver, take the next left. The shop I want is right down that street."

The shop had a lot of wares on the walk outside. Some people were buying with a haste that bespoke panic, as if there would be no more goods left when this day was over. We found the red curtains we wanted, and the kitchen utensils, and then Miss Cunningham got some worsted fabric, and the owner told us the store down the street was selling Brussels carpets for a dollar a yard and ingrain carpeting at seventy-five cents. So we went down the street, and she ordered the carpets and had them shipped to Mount Vernon.

"Immediately," she said, "lest traffic become dangerous on the river. Or they stop the boat to Mount Vernon."

There was about the whole affair an air of Christmas. We shopped all afternoon, taking the smaller items with us. *To think that I'm shopping for Mr. Washington's home*, I thought. And still I could not believe it.

On the way back to our hotel our driver told us that if

we had a spyglass, we would be able to see the Confederate flag. He pointed across the river to Virginia. "On top of a tavern in Alexandria."

When we got back to Willard's on Fourteenth Street, we found it becoming crowded. Uniformed attendants were busily welcoming guests, helping people out of hacks, grabbing portmanteaus. The slaves of the planters who had come for political reasons were waiting outside on the sidewalk. Bewhiskered, loudmouthed men and soldiers were all over the lobby.

It was late and we were glad to get back, and after bringing our purchases upstairs in the hotel, Miss Cunningham found we were just in time for the seven thirty tea, which wasn't a tea at all but boasted such delicacies as fried oysters, pâté de foie gras, blancmange, and dessert. The hotel was really filling up now.

"There will be many an agreement made over juleps in the bar this day," our waiter told us.

From my bed this night all I heard was the tread of men marching and the sound of fifes and drums. The moon made a white light on the Potomac. We'd heard that on the Virginia shore Southern regiments were establishing outposts.

And today we'd bought kitchen knives, a sieve, and a rolling pin for George Washington's kitchen.

"It is to be a place of neutral feeling, Mount Vernon,"

Miss Cunningham had told me at supper. I didn't think there was an ounce of neutral feeling anywhere in the Federal City, or anywhere this night. Under me I thought I felt the earth move.

I slept.

Three

Somehow the next morning we managed to get out of Washington. After breakfast, which included steak and onions as well as more fried oysters, we hailed another hack and piled our purchases in it. The attendants and clerks in the hotel were so filled up with themselves and their own importance in the crisis, you would think they had voted for secession of Virginia. They paid no mind to two ladies with packages. They obliged the important-looking gentlemen first.

But we got into our hack and made our way through the turmoil that was on the streets to the Sixth Street Wharf, to get the boat for Mount Vernon. There was a considerable tie-up in traffic right around the unfinished Washington Monument.

"What has happened?" Miss Cunningham asked the driver.

By now we had both figured out that hack drivers know more than Congress.

"Cattle fell into the canal," he said.

"Cattle?" I asked.

"The government had a whole herd grazing around the

monument. They're to feed the army. Something frightened them. Maybe a stray dog, and they made for the
water. Had to be fished out. Some drowned."

Now the cattle were being herded through the streets,
apparently ahead of us. So we didn't get to the wharf until
noon, and the morning boat had already left. We had to
wait two hours for the next one, but Miss Cunningham
wouldn't leave. She paid a small Nigra boy to guard our
possessions on the wharf, then we made our way to an
enchanting park nearby and sat down under some trees. A
vendor came by with ices and we bought some.

Soon the park began to fill up with soldiers, detoured in
their journey as we had been. Within a short time they gave
an impromptu regimental concert, and visitors wandered
over to sit on the grass and listen. Young women flirted
with the soldiers, children ran amongst them, and it soon
became a grand celebration. Some of the men had a great
cast-iron gun that they fired at targets in the river. Everyone became very excited. On the heels of all that came a
group of women handing out coffee and cake to the soldiers, and I was able to buy some for us.

"It's like a holiday," I said, "all over this city. Nothing but
flags and music and marching."

"I wonder if they all mind what it is for," Miss
Cunningham said.

We finally boarded the boat for Mount Vernon. Our
goods were stored, and except for some men bound for

Alexandria, whose Southern accents were very soft and thick, we were alone. They cast suspicious glances at us and we at them. *Everyone is suspicious of his neighbor now,* I thought. *Is that part of what makes war ugly? Nobody trusts anybody.*

We arrived at Mount Vernon at sunset, and I couldn't believe the sight.

The sun went to rest in back of the house, away from the river. There was now a pattern of broken-up purple clouds, through which the reddish orange light cast its glow.

The outline of the great house was black against the purple red sky. I knew it was in disrepair, but you couldn't see that from our boat. All you could see was the outline, the cupola on top, the great pillars, the chimneys and dormers, the trees, like a black-and-white sketch done by someone who loved the place.

I felt moved and stunned to inertia at the same time. The silhouette of General Washington's house against the brilliant red-and-purple sky was like a blessing on us. And we stood there staring at it like one would stare at the Sistine Chapel in Rome. *Unfathomable,* I thought. *That house is holding close its secrets.* And then I thought: *Those secrets need to be held now, and guarded, and at the same time shared with all the people. Maybe if we knew them, we wouldn't be so ready to fight one another.*

Then the captain rang the boat's bell. "Since 1812," he explained to us, "when the British burned the White

House, then came downriver past Mount Vernon and rang their bell out of respect for General Washington, every boat that passes or stops rings its bell."

I was exhausted, yet I felt things coming together for me. As if I belonged here. As if I'd been away too long and come home.

Four

Mr. Upton Herbert was a voice in the dusk to me, a strong hand to help me onto the half-sinking wharf, before he was a face or a person.

He'd seen our boat and come down to the wharf with a lantern, but wouldn't let the Nigra servants behind him stand on the wharf. "It's near falling in. One of the things I must repair as soon as possible," he said.

The lantern glow blinded me to his face, but his voice was firm and reassuring. As was the homey sound of frogs beeping, the smell of honeysuckle, and the sight of wild grapevines around the water's edge. Then we were going up the rickety steps to the lawn, and the servants were bringing our purchases.

Candles glowed in the windows of some rooms in the house. As we approached, it looked haunted.

"A room has been prepared for you," Mr. Herbert said to Miss Cunningham. "The downstairs bedroom that opens into the library. I figured we could furnish the library as your sitting room without compromising its purpose."

He was well spoken and educated. His voice had that tinge of musical Southern graciousness.

"Thank you," she said. "Tell the servants to be careful with that box. It holds my records and correspondence."

"The servants are Dandridge, Jane, Priscilla, and Emily," he said, introducing us. "And you are Miss Tracy?"

"You can call me Sarah."

We looked at each other. And I thought, *Why, he's as handsome as any of the men I've had as partners at dinner parties or soirees in Philadelphia, New York, or Maryland. What is he doing here? And in workman's clothing.* But I felt at ease with him because we had not been thrust on each other by well-meaning adults looking to make a match.

I can treat him as I want, I told myself. *I don't have to be sweet and charming. I can be myself.*

It occurred to me then that I did not know who myself was when it came to talking to a man. I had never been allowed to be myself.

"I have a room ready for you. It belonged to Jackie Custis, Mrs. Washington's son," he said.

"I'm honored," I told him.

"How did you find Washington City?"

"A bedlam," I told him. "Especially today."

"What happened today?"

"Why, Virginia seceded."

"Oh." He was silent for a moment. "Well, that will complicate things now. I won't be able to go to Washington City anymore. We don't get much news here until the *Collyer* comes."

"The *Collyer*?"

"The boat you were just on. As you can see, Captain Baker brought me the newspapers and mail, although I also get mail from Alexandria."

I had a question on my mind, but I couldn't ask it. The servants had brought our things inside the house, the first impression of which overwhelmed me. Candlelight flickered in the detached kitchen, from where the fragrance of coffee came, and beyond where we stood, the darkened rooms and stairway beckoned and loomed.

I felt small, lost, and unworthy. Had I done the right thing coming here?

"I'll show you to your room," Mr. Herbert said to Miss Cunningham. He was full of deference to her. I went into the kitchen after Priscilla.

"Would you like some coffee?" she asked.

"I'd love a cup," I said.

"I do it," another servant said. I think she was Emily. "I to be her personal maid."

"Mr. Herbert say no personal maids. Too much work for that," Priscilla shot back.

I could see immediately that they did not get on. They were both immaculately dressed and wore head turbans and had thick Southern accents. Were they slaves? Or paid? There was my question.

I could not have a servant who was a slave. Why hadn't I thought of that and brought my own girl? I'd left her at the

Maxwells' to help with the children. Travel made her physically sick, and besides, I hadn't wanted to upset the delicate balance of another's household.

"Jus' 'cause you the older don't make you smarter," Emily argued.

"I is older, an' Mama always say you're to listen to me."

So, they were sisters. That was all I needed to cast me down. People to remind me of home. "Anyone can give me the coffee," I said.

Mr. Herbert came back into the kitchen. "I'll have some too," he said.

I noticed the change in them when he came into the room. Right off they quieted down. Jane had gone to bed apparently. I'd seen her go up the stairway, to rooms above the kitchen. And Dandridge was still bringing our purchases into the hall.

"You two aren't fighting again," Mr. Herbert said.

"You said I to be her personal girl," Emily told him.

"I don't recall saying that, Emily, but if I did, is it a problem?"

"She jus' wanta hang around a fancy Northern lady and get *notions*," Priscilla told him.

I smiled. "I'm not fancy," I said.

"You is to me," Emily said.

Mr. Herbert sighed. I could get a better sense of him now. His face was pleasant. A strong nose and jaw, a firm chin, piercing blue eyes. He was clean shaven, no beard.

He managed to exude a gentle, cultured manner, yet you knew he was in full charge of things. "We'll discuss this in the morning. Emily, you may help Miss Tracy upstairs with her things. Everyone is tired."

Behind his back I actually saw Emily stick her tongue out at Priscilla. And I knew exactly how she felt. Then she started to bring my things up the stairs. Priscilla was indeed older and more mature. She looked as if you could depend on her. She shook her head sadly and went up the stairway in the kitchen.

I was left with Mr. Herbert.

"I'm sorry," he said.

"Mr. Herbert, I'm afraid I'm about to add to your woes."

"And why is that?"

"Are the Nigras unpaid?"

"Up to now they have been, yes. Mr. Washington left them here. Or to be more accurate, they refused to leave the place."

"Refused? Then, they are not slaves."

He smiled. "They consider themselves the children of Washington's slaves. It is a position to which they cling. As to your original question, I'm afraid they are unpaid."

"Then, how could they refuse to leave?"

His smile deepened. "I wouldn't expect you, as a Northerner, to understand."

"Well, as a Northerner, I can't have an unpaid Nigra waiting on me."

He sipped his coffee calmly.

I had heard that his great-grandmother was a daughter of William Fairfax, General Washington's neighbor. And that her sister married Lawrence Washington, the general's older half brother.

He stood so straight he might have had a sword at his side. Yet his hands had graceful movements. For one insane moment I saw him with a wig, breeches and a coat with buff facings, and a tricorn hat.

He sighed and ran a thumb across his brow. "They aren't paid, no. However, they are anything but slaves in the true sense of the word. They run the place. They make me crazy. They tell me what to do, for heaven's sake. And they are better clothed and fed than half the people in Fairfax County."

"That's the Southern way of thinking. Can they leave if they want to?"

He looked confused, as if the thought had never occurred to him. "I've already told you, they've refused to. Why would they want to?" he asked. "Who would feed them and look after them?"

"I can tell you're from Virginia," I said.

"Well, I don't deny it."

"I shall pay Emily if she is to wait on me." I knew I was being contentious.

"And then what will the others say?"

Now I had no answer for him. We looked at each other.

"I'm making trouble, aren't I?" I asked.

"Yes, you are."

"I'm from the North."

"I know, but I thought there were to be no sectional differences here at Mount Vernon."

"There already are," I said.

He nodded slowly, thoughtfully. "We'll ask Miss Cunningham," he said, "since the Association is running things now."

"She's from South Carolina," I reminded him.

"Then, if she says pay them, we shall. Agreed?"

"Agreed," I said.

"We'll discuss it in the morning," he said.

But in the morning we never did discuss it. In the morning a terrible thing happened. Mr. Herbert read in the newspapers that General Washington's body was no longer in its grave at the foot of the hill at Mount Vernon. But that it had been shipped out to the mountains of Virginia.

But I didn't know this when I went to sleep. The bed was made and the linens rough but clean, and somehow their roughness didn't bother me. So, this room had belonged to Jackie Custis.

What had I read about him? That he was the spoiled son of Martha and gave the general no end of headaches, being unable or unwilling to behave at school or study. That he married early and was not in the war but was at the surrender at Yorktown, where he contracted camp fever and died.

I felt no sense of him in the room. But as night closed in

and the house quieted I heard footfalls on the stairway and outside in the hall. Mr. Herbert had taken the Lafayette room. How did it feel to sleep where Lafayette had slept? I smiled, wondering what my sister, Fanny, would have to say, then turned over and fell asleep.

I woke to hear a clock downstairs strike eleven. Outside a hooty owl called. Then, again I heard steps in the hall, heavier than those of Mr. Herbert. Moonlight flooded my room. I got up, opened my door, and looked out into the hallway.

A man was walking there. A man in a long cape and boots, and holding a lighted candle.

Who was he? Certainly not Mr. Herbert! This man was heavyset and wore a planter's hat. I watched as he took a key from under his cape and opened the door of the room next to Mr. Herbert's. Then he went inside and the door closed.

It was not Upton Herbert. He did not have Mr. Herbert's easy yet purposeful walk. It was not Dandridge. I had seen that he was a white man.

Was he real, or was I imagining things?

Was he a ghost?

I was never one to give in to hysteria, not much on theatrics and didn't believe in ghosts. But just because you didn't believe, that didn't mean they didn't exist, did it?

Who was I to deny them existence?

I locked my door quickly and went back to bed.

Suppose he murdered us all in our sleep? Mr. Herbert had said nothing about another man in the house. At home in Troy we had a dog, a large, shaggy black-and-white dog named Pistol. And he'd never allow anyone to walk in our house at night like that without rousing the whole state of New York.

I lay awake a long time, listening to the owl calling, the silence, the faraway barking of a dog, and then I must have gone to sleep.

Five

*I*n the morning we had breakfast on the new striped oilcloth we had purchased in Washington City. The food was cooked by Jane, who did all the cooking. And that could be quite a bit, since I came down to see Mr. Herbert directing a bunch of men ready to work on the wharf. They were both black and white. And they all had to be fed a noon meal, which Jane took charge of.

"Did you all sleep well?" he asked.

"There's a man in the house," I said as Jane poured my coffee for me.

Mr. Herbert looked at me. "A man?"

"I saw him in the hall last night. I heard him. He went into the room at the end of the hall."

He and Jane stared at me.

"I don't see things," I insisted.

Mr. Herbert shook his head. His brow furrowed. He looked at his plate of eggs and ham. "I'm sorry he frightened you. That's Mr. Washington."

I and Miss Cunningham just stared at him.

He smiled apologetically. "John Augustine Washington. The man you all bought the house from. He keeps a room here. He has a farm nearby and uses the room when he visits his farm. I haven't been able to get him to leave."

"He just comes and goes as he pleases?" Miss Cunningham asked.

"I'm afraid so, yes," Mr. Herbert answered.

"That wasn't in the agreement," Miss Cunningham said. "We paid him for the house. He and his family officially moved out on the general's birthday last year. The only rights they maintain are to one quarter acre square surrounding the tomb. And they've agreed there will be no further burials within the vault."

"I know," Mr. Herbert answered. "I apologize for not being able to get him to leave. He's such a sad man. Lost his wife only last month and he's left with six children. I'm afraid this house means a precious lot to him."

Miss Cunningham sighed. "It must be difficult for him to let go of this place. They lived here so long. But still, he cannot keep coming and going. He must make the break."

"Yes," Mr. Herbert agreed.

"Is he still sleeping?" I asked.

"I'm afraid he is, yes," Mr. Herbert answered. "Unlike his famous ancestor, he does sleep late."

"Then, I'll speak to him, if it's all right with you all. I mean, I'll speak to him in Miss Cunningham's place. In the name of the Association."

Was I treading on Mr. Herbert's toes again? He seemed about to say something, then agreed. "Fine. But I'm afraid there's another matter that should have your attention this morning, Miss Cunningham. And it's far less pleasant."

And then he opened the *New York Herald*. "I just got this yesterday." He showed us the article.

It told about General Washington's body no longer residing in the vault at Mount Vernon.

"What?" Miss Cunningham said. "Are my eyes finally going? It cannot be."

"It's the press wreaking havoc with us," Mr. Herbert said.

The poor lady was distraught by now. She walked the floor in the kitchen. She spoke sharply to the servants, ordering them out. She spilled over her cup of coffee on her black grosgrain dress. I had to help her to a chair in the library and get her another cup of coffee to soothe her nerves.

"Who would move the body?" she asked, and I could tell the thought was too horrible for her to conceive.

"They're saying Mr. John Augustine," Mr. Herbert told her.

"Well, you see?" she said, as if the natural outcome of allowing him to come around was talk of the body being removed. "If he weren't here at all, the rumor would not have started. There are people out there, Mr. Herbert, who will do anything at all to blacken the name of the Association. I know most all the newspapers are against what we're doing here. A lot of it has to do with the fact that I am regent and I'm from South Carolina."

"Well, I'm superintendent and I'm from Virginia."

"They call me Secesh." I could hear the pain in her voice. "I'd resign, but it would only open a Pandora's box. Some of the women who would take my place would cause all kinds of mischief. I'm afraid the only paper with us is the *Intelligencer*."

"Then, have them print a response. Invite them to come and see that the vault hasn't been touched. By God, what rot!" Mr. Herbert was angry.

"Mrs. Lincoln calls them the vampire press. Now I know why," Miss Cunningham said.

I saw my chance then. My chance to prove to both of them that I could face problems head-on. "I'll take care of it," I said.

They both looked at me then.

"Haven't you enough with Mr. Washington?" Mr. Herbert asked.

"It's my job," I said firmly. And it was. Miss Cunningham agreed. I would write the letter that very morning. I turned to get pen and paper.

"Mr. Herbert," Miss Cunningham said to Mr. Herbert, "you must make me a promise here and now that you will not join the army. I know your two brothers are serving, but you must promise me, please."

I heard him promise her. I went to write the letter.

"We are requested by the ladies of the Mount Vernon Association to state that the assertation which appeared in the *New York Herald* of the 15th instant to the effect that Col. J. A. Washington had caused the removal of the remains of General Washington from Mount Vernon is utterly false and without foundation," I wrote.

And: "The public, the owners of this noble possession, need fear no molestation of this one national spot belonging alike to North and South."

Now that Virginia has seceded, we expect to hear any day that the mails have been stopped. But as Mr. Herbert says, there is always the Adams Express Company. He went that afternoon to take my letter to Alexandria.

After I wrote the letter, I spoke with Mr. John Augustine Washington.

I found him in the kitchen. He was having a late breakfast. He was a large, clumsy-looking man, cleanly but carelessly dressed. He stood up when I came in, almost knocking over the chair he'd been sitting in.

"Mr. Washington." I felt false saying it. Surely this man, so slovenly, so awkward, who slept late and crept about like a thief in this house, could not be descended from the stern, disciplined General Washington. Why, John Augustine looked so sad.

"I'm Sarah Tracy," I told him. "From the Association."

"Miss Tracy." He bowed.

"You frightened me when you came in last night."

"I'm sorry," he said.

I got right to it. "Mr. Herbert tells me you often come and go at odd hours. Are you intending to keep the room upstairs indefinitely, Mr. Washington?"

"No, ma'am. Only until I can make other arrangements."

It was the first time ever that I'd been called ma'am, and it shook me. "We, that is, the Association wants to repair and clean the whole house. It would be so much easier without tenants. I'm sure you understand."

Oh, he understood, all right. He understood that he was being asked to leave by a slip of a girl with a Northern accent. For good.

He understood that his time here, and that of his family, was finished. An era was over. Did I see an even deeper shade of sadness come over the round, perplexed face? It must feel terrible to be thrown out of one's own house!

He bowed again. "I have some last-minute things to pack up, and then I'll be out, Miss Tracy," he said. "But there is just one final thing I'd like to do."

"Yes, what is that?"

"I'd like to throw my key to the general's tomb in the river. Since I heard about how I was supposed to have removed his body."

That startled me, put me off balance. But I recovered. "Of course," I said.

"I'd like to do it today. Before I leave."

"Yes."

"Would you accompany me to the wharf to do it? That way you can testify to the public, if need be, that I no longer have access to the tomb."

Oh, I felt things breaking inside me. What had I started here? Miss Semple had always told us to be careful with words in our lives. For we could set things in motion. What had I set in motion?

"Of course I'll accompany you," I said. "And thank you, Mr. Washington. The Association thanks you." I turned to go. Then stopped. "We offer our regrets for the loss of your wife."

"Yes," he said.

He would hate me. The only man walking around with the Washington name would hate me, I decided. And with every right. I had, after all, just dismissed him. I could see his confusion, his sorrow, his embarrassment.

And I knew that if he'd looked and acted at all like the general, I wouldn't have been able to do it. But he didn't. And I think that's why I was so horrible. I was angry at him for being slovenly, for eating breakfast late, for sleeping late, for letting the house go into disrepair, for *not being like his ancestor*!

I went with him that day to the shaky wharf so he could throw his key in the river. I had explained to Mr. Herbert, so the workmen all stepped back on the land and gathered to watch.

I felt there should be a ceremony or something. After

all, it was an official good-bye from John Augustine Washington, the last of them, to Mount Vernon. It was, if you will, a changing of the guard. But there were no soldiers, no guns, no sharply called orders, there was no marching.

There was only a moment's silence on everybody's part and the plop of the key in the water. Then more silence as we watched the ripples. And then we moved away.

Mr. Washington moved out that day. And I, oh, I proved my mettle to Mr. Herbert and Miss Cunningham, didn't I? I had met the situation head-on and handled it. Then, why did I feel so bad? Why did I hate myself?

Two days later my letter appeared in the *Intelligencer*. We didn't see the paper, however, until the day after, and when I saw it, I was both proud and ashamed. There was my name in print! There were my words.

Washington's body was still at Mount Vernon, I told everybody. But his awkward, confused descendent I have thrown out.

Mr. Herbert finally found time to give me a tour of the house. With the exception of some things brought from his own house, the only things left in it from the general are the bust of him done by Houdon, the terrestrial globe in his study, and the key to the Bastille given to him by Lafayette.

This house has about it the musty sadness of a house

with memories. They cling in corners. I cannot walk up or down the stairs but I think: *George Washington once walked on these very stairs. I am walking in his footsteps.*

Will I ever get over feeling as if I am on sacred ground?

I must ask Mr. Herbert one day, after we finish arguing about the help getting paid. For that still clings to the air between us.

But the house also has a pulse. I can feel it beating, though softly. It asks to be taken for no more than it is right now, an empty, echoing shell. And I sense it is grateful for our presence. It seems, at times, almost apologetic for the trouble it is causing us.

It seems like John Augustine Washington. I think of him often. And with sadness and guilt.

Mr. Herbert constantly talks about refurbishing. The first room he wants to tackle is Mr. Washington's bedroom. He has asked Miss Cunningham for permission to plaster, paper, and paint, as if you could plaster, paper, and paint over memories. He says that if the room had been in order all along, he could have paid a man to guard it and made money besides. Could you just see a man with nothing to do all day but guard General Washington's room?

Sometimes I think Mr. Herbert has notions.

He expects visitors and says we will be able to make money from them. He knows where to get some chairs. From the Lewises, who are kin to Washington. He says they are breaking up housekeeping.

On the other hand, we are lucky to have him. He knows everybody around here. I suppose notions aren't the worst thing a man can have.

He also says the sills in the house will last three or four years, but the roof can no longer be delayed. It is leaking and will ruin everything inside.

The wind was very bad last night, and in it I heard many children's voices. It carried away the covered passage from the house to the kitchen. I thought I heard children laughing as if they were doing great mischief.

It is the twenty-fifth of May and the season is so lovely that I want to fill my eyes with the sights and smells every day. The strawberry vines and fruit trees are laden, and we are already eating asparagus. Everything has blossomed and the greenery is a feast for the eyes. I am starting a small kitchen garden off to the side in back of the house. And I cannot live without flowers. There are some beautiful roses blooming here from years past, and yesterday Mr. Herbert went into Alexandria and got me eight dollars more in seeds. But the news from everywhere is terrible.

On the nineteenth of April, Union troops traveling through Baltimore on their way to duty in the capital were fired upon and stoned by a mob of civilians. It was the exact day that the fighting started up at Lexington and Concord in General Washington's war. There has to be some connection in that. Does nobody see it but me?

Earlier this month Alexandria was in turmoil. Union troops marched in to take it from the Confederates. The town was wild with excitement, Mr. Herbert said. He was there. A twenty-four-year-old colonel from New York's Fire Zouaves strode right into the Marshall House, went to the upper story, and took down the Confederate flag, and as he came down the stairs Mr. Jackson, who owns the place, stopped him with a blast from a shotgun. The dead soldier's name was Elmer Ellsworth. The Fire Zouaves wear their hair shorn under large red caps and carry big bowie knives. Their behavior, in general, is very wild.

Another Zouave shot Jackson dead. Mr. Herbert said the blood of Jackson and Ellsworth ran together on the stairs.

He saw it as they were bringing out the bodies. He was very shaken when he came home. Ellsworth's body was laid in state in the East Room of the White House, because he was a personal friend of the Lincolns'.

Mr. Herbert made a final trip to Alexandria, aware of the fact that it is now under Union leadership. It was very sad for him. He will not take the test oath, so he will be unable to go there anymore. His brother has a bank there, and he'd pick up the mail and go shopping.

This time he brought a letter for Miss Cunningham. Her mother is ill and she is needed at home immediately.

~

It was about five days ago that he brought the letter. That night we sat at supper in the kitchen and stared at one another.

"I cannot leave here," Miss Cunningham said dully.

"And why not?" I was careful to be chipper and stout of purpose.

"Because." She hesitated then and looked from me to Mr. Herbert and back at me again. "It isn't seemly, leaving you here without a chaperone."

Mr. Herbert had the grace to blush. I didn't.

"This is a time of war," I told her. "All kinds of unseemly things are going to happen. Look at what happened in Alexandria to that poor Colonel Ellsworth! Anyway, we have the servants. I can't get a minute's peace away from Emily or Priscilla. Why, they're living right in the house with us."

She sighed. "Yes, you are right about that. But I don't want any shadow of suspicion cast on this project."

"They've already cast shadows," Mr. Herbert reminded her, "with this business about Washington's body. Go home, Miss Cunningham. We can stand firm in the face of whatever comes."

She finally agreed. If I would put an ad in the Alexandria paper advertising for a woman to come and stay. If I would write to my friend Mary McMakin, in Philadelphia, and ask her to come.

I didn't want to do either one, but I promised I would. I wanted to be the mistress of Mount Vernon.

We talked, too, about paying or not paying the Nigras.

I brought it up before she left.

"Why, of course we will pay them," Miss Cunningham said. "I have it in the budget to pay them."

Mr. Herbert and I looked at each other.

"Why do you seem confused?" she asked.

"You are from South Carolina," I managed to say.

"We thought . . . ," said Mr. Herbert, and he waved a hand to dismiss the thought.

"You thought that because I own slaves, I would not pay for these people. But they are not my people," she said. "And the Association must pay them. Or we will be criticized. It is very important, Mr. Herbert. They must be recompensed for their services. Do you hear?"

"I hear," he said.

"Then, they are free?" I asked.

But that would be taking it too far. For both of them.

"They work for us," Miss Cunningham said simply.

"They won't go anywhere," Mr. Herbert promised.

But were they free? I knew that to push the point would be to create chaos here. And what we were doing, keeping Mount Vernon in order, was more important right now than creating chaos.

So I kept silent. For the moment.

~

I had to help Miss Cunningham pack, then Dandridge drove us to Alexandria. I stayed in Alexandria with her until she boarded her boat. "I will be back soon," she said, "I promise."

The trip home, for me, was uneventful.

Six

*H*ere are some of the things that have happened so far in June.

Mr. Herbert had to dismiss a man for drinking, and we found he was in Alexandria sending bad messages to the men here, trying to get them to leave our employ.

I received a box of preserves and orange syrup from Mother.

Mr. Herbert had two washstands in his room and he gave me one.

Dandridge was stopped and searched when he brought a load of cabbages to Alexandria to sell. How could they be suspicious of Dandridge? He is gentlemanly and efficient, our all-around man. I would trust him with my life.

All the rooms have been swept and cleaned, even in the garret. I wanted to cut some carpet for the rooms upstairs, but the workmen were sanding that side of the house and had all the windows closed, and I did not have enough light.

A man in Alexandria is making us a simple but rich single bedstead for fourteen dollars. And a tufted haircloth mahogany chair for thirteen dollars. Mr. Herbert has a black walnut dining-room extension table in his house that we may borrow. He has brought other items from his house. He calls his place Bleak House. It seems to fit him somehow. He is so very proper. I don't know why Miss Cunningham worried about leaving us together. We work well together, respect and understand each other. Of course, I have not told my people at home yet that she has left. I think Fanny would get on the first train and come right down and fetch me. Well, good that there is a war on, then. Aren't there such things as enemy lines? If not, there soon will be, and she will be unable to come by the time I tell her Miss Cunningham has left. If I ever do.

We must buy some dining-room chairs.

I have gotten a woman to come in once a week to do the washing.

The house sits between the Federal pickets at Arlington and the Confederate muster point at Manassas Junction. A Union commander is said to be occupying Robert E. Lee's house at Arlington, and roads have been made, trees cut down, and earthworks dug all around Lee's place. I understand it was once very beautiful and that when she left, Mrs. Lee was crying.

We paid the servants, finally, one day in June.

"What this be for?" Priscilla asked as Mr. Herbert put the money in her hand. He had assembled them in the foyer, and Priscilla was the first one to feel the money.

"It's your pay," he said.

In each hand he put some money. And they were in wonderment, like children on Christmas Day.

"We kin spend this?" Dandridge asked.

"Yes, you may spend it," Mr. Herbert told them.

"I save mine," Emily said. She pressed the hand with the money in it close to her breast. "I heared about slaves who buy their own freedom."

Mr. Herbert and I looked at each other significantly. He appeared to be uncomfortable then and had to clear his throat, and he said something noble to them about how dear they were to him. But neither he nor I said that one of these days their freedom would be given to them. Or that slaves didn't get paid. Or that, for all intents and purposes, they were free now.

Or that the only reason they weren't was because he and I were more confused about the issue than a mule in a mud hut.

I should have said something, as a representative of the Association. I know Miss Cunningham would have wanted me to. But I thought it was Mr. Herbert's job. And besides that, I was too much of a prissy boots to begin with.

I feel like a nest-building bird. What kind of bird, I don't know. I think I would like to be a cardinal because then my husband's coat would be bright red.

Speaking of birds, the house has already given me gifts.

I have a pet crow who comes around out back near my vegetable garden and lights on the brick fence around it. Mr. Herbert says he must repair the fence. The workmen around here make their own bricks.

I didn't know crows could be so tame. He looks at me with bright eyes and bobs and weaves to get my attention. I give him some bread from the kitchen scraps, and he stays around while I weed the garden. Then he flies away.

"Didn't you know crows can be harbingers of bad news?" Mr. Herbert asked me.

"Now, that seems like a Southern belief," I told him. "In Troy we don't think that way. Can't they also be friendly?"

He scowled. "Obviously this one intends to be." But his scowl was friendly. I think he is often amused by me.

The other gift is the sight of a resident eagle who soars amongst the trees down by the river. Mr. Herbert has been working on the wharf, repairing it, and I have been down there several times watching. He has taken a small boat out to fish for shad, and then he has cooked it as only he knows how.

I am not much of a cook. At home the kitchen belonged to Mother, and my job was to set the table. We had one housemaid, Ella, a silent, disapproving person who set standards I could never possibly meet.

I have, in proper order, written to my friend Mary McMakin, in Philadelphia, and asked her to come and be my chaperone.

She wrote back and said her mother was ill and she could not come at the moment.

I have put the ad in the Alexandria paper to find a girl to come and stay with me. It seems so silly. What will I do with her when she comes? Am I not telling Upton Herbert that I do not trust him by doing this?

"You must do as you are told," he admonished me. He was standing on the wharf, tamping some tobacco into his pipe for a moment's relaxation. The river and the Maryland shore were behind him. Quite a backdrop. And now that I have been around him for a while, I can describe Mr. Herbert better. He is a lean, brown-eyed man, with the grace of hundreds of years of breeding in his movements. He dresses in brown. His shirts and fingernails are always clean.

"You speak to me as if I'm a child," I said.

"Aren't you still?"

"I'm a woman of twenty-two."

"If that is your claim."

"What mean you by that, sir?"

He smiled. "Don't get on your high horse, but if you're twenty-two, I'm Napoléon's nephew."

"Do you accuse me of lying?"

"Just stretching the truth a bit for your own ends."

"I'm twenty-two."

He drew a letter out of his coat pocket. "I have proof here that states otherwise."

My heart dropped inside me. I reached for the letter, but he pulled back.

"Who is it from?" I asked.

"Mrs. Francis Knudson."

I gasped. "My sister, Fanny? She wrote to you? On what pretext?"

"Just to tell me that you are only eighteen."

"Oh!" I had no words. I had only anger, then feelings of betrayal and hurt. "She had no right. She's always tried to hurt me and stop me from doing things. Oh, the witch."

"Now, now, she's an older sister."

"I hate her. She's ruined everything for me."

"Nothing is ruined," he said. "The information will go no further."

I hesitated a moment. "Why would you do that for me?"

"Because I think you are right for the job. You belong here, as do I. You appreciate the place for what it is."

How could I be angry at that assessment? Oh, he had me so confused. I turned to look up at the house. "I feel as if I belong here," I said.

"And so you do. I've seen some of your letters to Miss Cunningham. They seem to echo Mr. Washington's when he was away at war, writing home."

"They do?"

"Yes. I'll show you how they resemble each other sometime."

"But what will we do about Fanny?"

He thought for a moment. "I'll write to her and tell her I'll take the matter up with Miss Cunningham and we'll abide by her wishes."

"You'd lie for me?"

"I can tell a judicious lie sometimes. Look, we're at war. You are settled in here. Miss Cunningham's health is fragile, and anyway, she can't travel through the lines now. It would be worse not to lie at this point. Ohh. I think we have guests." He laid down his hammer and ruler and nails. "Soldiers."

They were from the Union army. Five of them. They explained they were stationed near here and wanted to see Washington's tomb. One was a boy of only about seventeen. "Want to see if he's still here," he said.

I saw in Mr. Herbert's face and demeanor the angry superintendent warring with the Southern gentleman, and I stepped in.

"I'll gladly show it to you," I said, "if you check your guns here at the gate and put on other clothing."

"We're Union, ma'am. And we don't give up our arms."

"I don't want your old arms," I answered. "I wouldn't know what to do with them. But I ask you to respect the dead and the fact that this place is neutral ground."

"By whose order?" the only officer with them said.

"General Winfield Scott," I lied.

"Well, we don't have other clothes, ma'am," the officer said.

"Then, wait here. I'll go into the house and get something

for you to cover your markings of rank with. That is the only way you can approach General Washington's tomb, I'm afraid."

I sounded braver than I felt. But they waited. I ran into the house and, seeing Emily in the hall, grabbed the shawl from around her shoulders. "Go and find me four more," I ordered.

"What you doin' with my shawl?" she asked.

"Never mind, I'll return it immediately. Do as I say."

In several minutes she came back with four more shawls. Two were mine. I ran outside again and down to where the soldiers were standing with Mr. Herbert. Would grown men agree to put shawls around their shoulders like little old ladies? Would they agree to leave their guns at the gate?

"Gentlemen." I held up the shawls.

"You can't expect me to put that on, ma'am," the youngest soldier said.

"And why not?"

"It's like my granny wears."

"Respect," I said. "If I had blankets enough, I'd give you those. Just pretend they are blankets. And think of the story you'll have to tell your grandchildren. You actually visited George Washington's tomb."

There was some mumbling, but they took the shawls and draped them around their shoulders. "Anybody tell anybody back in camp about this an' you're dead meat," the officer threatened.

"We all got the same secret," one of the others said.

They left their guns and we went down the hill to Washington's tomb. We stood outside the cast-iron gate reflectively. They took off their hats.

"Just wanted to pay our respects, sir," the officer said.

Tears came to my eyes. Overhead I heard my eagle calling. If I were given to conjure, like the Nigras, I'd say it was a sign. But I am a good Yankee, believing in no such nonsense.

At the top of the hill again, they handed back the shawls, offered Mr. Herbert some money, and picked up their rifles. "Thank you, ma'am," the youngest one said.

As we watched them walk away Upton looked at me. "I told you you belonged here," he said, "but you'd better get the matter official. With General Scott, I mean."

As my eagle soared gracefully overhead I promised him I would. I was flush with success. I felt as if I could accomplish anything.

Seven

I have met some of the neighbors. I think they are all Quakers, although we have one foot-washing Baptist in the person of Mrs. Jean Harbinger. She came around one day bearing a pecan pie. She is a tall, sad woman who lost one son when he fell from a horse and broke his neck. She came with another, named Robert. He is about seventeen and completely under his mother's domination. She should send him away to school instead of keeping him wrapped around her like a shawl.

She wears grief on her like a shawl too. It even shows in her walk, which is languid and reluctant, as if she really has no place to go and nothing to look forward to.

She is the one who told me we are surrounded by a Quaker settlement. That all of George Washington's farms were purchased by Quakers.

"He hated Quakers," she told me, as if she knew him personally. "They thwarted all his war aims in the Jersey legislature. You watch. The ones around here won't be found if there is trouble in the neighborhood. They'll hide in their cellars."

"That isn't quite right, Mother," Robert told her. "There

are a lot of Quakers who have sons in gray right now. And some who have sons in blue."

She told him to hush. I made her tea, and she spoke of her boy Donnie as if he were still with her. Then she spoke about the neighborhood.

"Many Quaker Friends fled to New Jersey when it looked like there was going to be war," she said, "but they have all returned. The big house on Union Farm, half a mile from your west gate, has been reopened. And there are lights on at Walnut Hill."

She knew everything about the neighborhood. Then she told me about old Wes Ford, an ex-slave man who is living nearby.

"He came to your mansion about 1802," she said. "When Bushrod Washington inherited the place from the general. And he left with John Augustine's family. He stayed that long, though he'd been set free in his master's will in 1829. One thing about the Nigras around here. They don't want to leave. Robert, pour me another cup of tea."

He poured it.

"So Mr. Herbert told me," I said.

"Wes Ford can tell stories about the general and his wife. Stories told to him by Billy, the general's body servant himself. Billy was still living here when Wes Ford came in 1802."

Then, having won my interest, she gave the conversation a turn.

"Funny, isn't it? You and Mr. Herbert living all alone here in this big house."

"Mr. Herbert is going to start a Home Guard. I'm going to ask him to teach me how to shoot," Robert said.

"Robert, you are not going to learn how to shoot. Now, we have discussed this."

"We're not alone," I said. Robert's young, handsome face was flushed. He reminded me of Charles, my first love.

"Oh? I'd heard that the lady from the Association had a sick mother. Didn't she go home to her?"

I was trapped. "Yes, she did. But we have four servants, three of them women. And I'm actively seeking a female companion." I looked at her. "Do you want the job?"

"I beg your pardon?"

"Do you want to come and live here with me and help guard my virtue?"

She looked flustered. "Dear me, no. I'm not insinuating anything. I don't wish you to take it that way. Heavens, I've known Mr. Herbert for years. We all have. He is so full of decorum he could pass for Saint Joseph in the dark."

I had never liked Saint Joseph. I didn't think much of a man who'd allow angels to tell him how to conduct his marriage.

Then she got up. "Come, Robert, it is time to go." She turned to me. "The good Lord has his plan. I'm sure you will find someone."

"I'm sure I will."

"He knew what he was doing when he took my Donnie. At least Donnie won't have to go fight in the war and get himself killed."

I did not understand such convoluted reasoning. But then, I did not know how a mother felt who had lost a son. I did know that if it happened to me, I wouldn't go around telling people that the Lord knew what he was doing. And I wouldn't make my other son pay for it either.

The next who came to visit was Anne Frobel, a Quaker woman.

She came the day I was planning on going to town to get passes for myself and the servants.

"Is thee planning a trip?"

"I was going to Alexandria to get passes."

"And why isn't Mr. Herbert taking thee?"

"He's been advised against going."

"Ah, so he hasn't taken the loyalty oath, then?"

"No, he hasn't, Mrs. Frobel."

"Well, we Quakers don't take oaths, you know. But I did come to deliver him a message."

I had brought her into the kitchen and sat her down. "Shall I fetch him? He's repairing the wharf."

"No, but thee can tell him this. We got together and decided that if he needs our men in the Home Guard he is starting in the neighborhood, they are willing to serve."

I stared blankly at her. "But I thought . . . ," I said, and then I stopped.

She smiled. "Mrs. Harbinger was here, then?"

I smiled. "Yes."

"She's trouble, that woman. Here, let me cut the rhubarb pie. It's from rhubarb in my own garden. Everybody thinks we hide in time of trouble, Miss Tracy. We don't go looking for it, is all. But when it comes, we don't try to sidestep it. Already two boys from the neighborhood have joined the Union army."

I nodded. "I'm neutral, Mrs. Frobel," I told her. "So I quite understand your feelings. We want to keep this place neutral ground. Open to all."

"As it should be," she agreed solemnly.

I consider it beyond the pale that Mr. Herbert cannot go to Alexandria anymore. It would hurt me terribly if I were home on my father's farm and couldn't go into Troy. I know Mr. Herbert is pained because of this, especially since he is known by everyone in the county as an upstanding man with a strong central core, something planted there inside him by his ancestors, who carved out this country before it was a country.

Lest it sound as if I am mooning over him, that is not the case. We have a professional friendship.

It is late June now. Except for the soldiers who come to visit in small groups once in a while, one wouldn't even think there was a war going on. I know I have to go to Washington City to see General Scott, to get passes for our servants, but

I don't want to disrupt the lazy peace of the days.

We seem to have established a pattern in the house. I get up early, but no matter how early, it seems as if Mr. Herbert is in the kitchen at breakfast already. He asks, at breakfast, if there is anything I need done in and about the place that day. And I ask him about food. What is coming into bloom in the fields? Are the corn and potatoes and tomatoes ready? Would he like fish for supper? If so, does he want to take the boat out or have Dandridge do it? If I'm going to town, I ask him if there is anything he wants. Then we part, he going his way and I, mine. I assign the servants their jobs, decide what I am going to do, and, if I need help, ask them to assist me.

I check their work during the day, visit my garden, cast some bread crumbs to my crow, feed the chickens, put milk out for the cat, and in general behave like a housewife who is seeing well to the ways of her household.

Mr. Herbert insists that if I go to town, I take Emily with me. "There are soldiers wandering around out there on the roads and in the woods," he reminds me.

Every day, no matter what happens, I write a letter to Miss Cunningham and report happenings and expenditures. I have not heard from her since she left. I wonder when she is coming back and almost hope she isn't.

This first week in July, Mr. Herbert did not want to talk about fish or money at breakfast.

"There are rumors," he said, "that Federal troops might be placed here."

I stared at him. "And from whence come these rumors?"

"A Nigra friend of Dandridge's came around yesterday. It's all the talk in Alexandria, he said."

"Can you trust him?"

"Yes."

"All right, then I must go today to see General Scott and tell him we will not have Federal troops here, mustn't I?"

He regarded me sadly. "Take Priscilla. She's a better bodyguard than Emily. You know how Emily is afraid of war."

"I think Emily is the only sane one amongst us," I told him.

"Be serious, Miss Tracy."

"Do you think there is any sanity at all in our being here?"

"Miss Cunningham insists that the presence of a lady will keep people from looting and destroying this place."

I laughed. Then I sobered. "So, Mr. Herbert, I'm to hold off the maddening hordes."

"So far it's worked. And I wish you'd call me Upton, not Mr. Herbert."

"Then, you must call me Sarah."

"Agreed."

I betook myself to Washington City. I went by the

omnibus from Alexandria, taking Priscilla with me because Emily was making pies and was afraid of war.

Priscilla is one person I would describe as stout of purpose. It makes her appear matronly, though I know she is not yet thirty. Emily is thin and filled with nervous excitement. Priscilla knows most everyone in the neighborhood, and though she wears a turban, I know she has gray in her hair.

Emily has a monstrous fear of the war, but I think Priscilla would meet a contingent of soldiers head-on and scold them for having dirty boots. In the pecking order of things, I know she considers herself senior servant in the house, and I let her have the privilege.

Washington City was in the same state as the last time we were there, only more so. Soldiers marching, crowds shuffling, soldiers cooking and eating on government lawns, Nigras holding horses' reins and waiting outside hotels, boys screeching headlines.

"We must go to the War Department," I told Priscilla.

"They gots a whole department for that? My, my," she said, "these white people do take on about things."

Yes, I thought as we wended our way through glass doors and across marble floors, *we do take on, don't we?*

The man I must see first, to be proper about things, was a Mr. Graham, a friend of Miss Cunningham's. In no time we found his office, but he was not in. So I turned to the officer who had ushered us to his door. "Take me to

General Scott," I said, and I explained to him who I was and why I had come.

"Miss, we can't just barge in on General Scott."

"You just take me there. I'll tend to the barging."

We went up another flight of stairs. There were soldiers and men standing all over the place, likely waiting to see the general too, but they parted like the Red Sea for Moses when we came through. The hall was large, echoing, and dimly lit, and the tiled floor was dirty from so many boots.

On a door was printed his name: GENERAL WINFIELD SCOTT. The officer knocked and, from inside, was told to enter. He went in, leaving the door slightly ajar.

"A friend of Miss Cunningham's," I heard a deep, booming voice say. "What does she want?"

I did not hear the reply, but I heard laughter. Then, "God bless the ladies!" And the door opened and they came out.

General Scott was in full uniform, with gold epaulets on his shoulders and a double row of brass buttons in front. He was gray haired, and tufts of hair stood out over his ears.

"My dear lady, I can promise you that no Federal troops will be stationed or placed at Mount Vernon," he said. "Nor will they march across its lawns with guns."

"Thank you," I said. "We wish to keep the place free of war. A neutral ground."

"As behooves its sacred atmosphere," he said. "But now"—and there was a twinkle in his eye—"can you be equally sure Virginia will honor this agreement?"

He was asking me to speak for Virginia! For the Southern army! So I did.

"Yes," I said. "I can."

Thank heaven he did not ask me how. For I did not know the how of it. He bowed, took my hand, and kissed it. "God bless the ladies," he said again. "You are a refreshing appearance in my long and terrible day. I shall give you a written order."

"And I'll need a pass for myself and the servants."

"That, too," he agreed.

I have met the commander in chief of the Northern army, I thought as we went back downstairs. *And he made me a promise. I wonder what Fanny would have to say about that. I wonder what Mother and Father would have to say.*

Then I thought, *But he is old. Mr. Lincoln wanted Robert E. Lee, but he went with the South instead. Mr. Lincoln will not keep General Scott as commander in chief for long. But he is that now. And he met with me. Me! And I have his word, his order, and no one shall doubt me.*

Eight

*T*wo days later a letter came from the Accotink post office, the closest to Mount Vernon. It was from a Mrs. Merrick, written for Mrs. Lincoln! Addressed to me!

My hands shook as I opened it. Everyone stood around, just inside the front door, in the foyer.

Was she going to rescind General Scott's order? Remonstrate with me? Why did I regard her as my older sister, Fanny? Why was I afraid?

"Oh!" My hand flew to my mouth. "She wants to come here! She wants to see Mr. Washington's home! Oh dear!"

The others became all excited. I regarded it with dismay.

"What is it?" Upton asked me when the servants had left the foyer.

"I can't meet with her."

"But why?"

"It would be construed as a political act."

"Meeting the wife of the president?"

"As a representative of the Association, I can't greet the wife of the president of the United States. That was one thing Miss Cunningham told me to keep in mind, not to favor one side over the other."

"In heaven's name, meeting the woman would be favoring the North over the South?" He was incredulous.

I sat down on the nearest chair. "I'm afraid so."

"Well then, what do we do? Tell her she can't come?"

"No," I said, "but I'm afraid you'll have to meet with her."

"But she knows you are the lady in residence here."

"Does she?" I asked bleakly.

"Believe me, everybody in Washington knows by now. What will you be doing, then, while I meet with her?"

"Hiding," I said.

He smiled. He does have a lovely smile. "I have to admire your gift for politics."

"It isn't a gift. It's common sense. First thing you know, I'd have the Southern regents on me. Then the newspapers."

He sighed. "Well then, I'll do the honors. I'll meet with her and take her on the tour. You had best be out of sight."

What if she knows of me? I wondered. *What if she and General Scott have spoken? What will he think? Will he go back on his word and send troops here?*

Is this what politics is? I asked myself. *If so, I hate it. It's a dirty men's business.*

If the Federals run the war the way they have run this expedition for Mrs. Lincoln, they will most likely lose. Mrs.

Merrick requested use of our boat for Mrs. Lincoln and her party. I said absolutely not.

Mrs. Merrick wrote back a rather nasty note, reminding me how full the boat would be with important people. And that we might, considering the poverty they heard we were in, like some of that Republican gold! The nerve.

I wrote and said no again. If Mrs. Lincoln came, she must come as an ordinary person. Furthermore, it should be kept out of the papers and not made into a circus.

Where am I getting the mettle for this? I don't know. Where does one get the mettle for anything?

I don't like Mrs. Lincoln anyway. Not many people do. They say she is bossy and short and fat and acts like Cleopatra and that she makes poor Mr. Lincoln crazy.

I shall develop a dreadful cold in my bones and go and see Dr. Anderson in Alexandria on the day they arrive.

It rained today. So they couldn't come.

The Lincoln boys have the measles, so another note has come round saying they can't come.

They came today. I took some cabbages and some roses to town to sell and went to Dr. Anderson and got some medicine for my cold.

Upton served as host. He welcomed them. He of the impeccable Virginia manners. He showed them the banquet hall, George Washington's bedroom, the gardens. He gave them the royal tour and shared his own humble supper with them, his ham and potatoes and vegetables.

He is a real Virginian, and I am sure politics never came up. But then, Mrs. Lincoln is a Southerner herself, with two brothers in the Confederate army. I am sure they got along.

Still, I can't believe that Upton did this.

I must laugh. If I do not laugh, I shall cry.

I have received a letter from Mother. "We did so want you at the Maxwells' this summer," she wrote. "They have a wonderful nephew who is going to visit them, and Mrs. Maxwell has told him all about you. He can't wait to meet you, and now you are off on your own. Fanny is very worried about you. She threatens to come and bring you home."

Fanny, indeed! She has never bestirred herself out of Troy. Doesn't she know there is a war on? I must write and tell them about the enemy lines.

Oh, I am so angry!

I think of what I have done this day.

I went on a made-up visit to a doctor to avoid seeing the wife of the president of the United States.

I had to make the decision not to see Mrs. Lincoln on my own because of the political implications. And Fanny threatens to come and rescue me! As I said, I must laugh or I shall cry.

~

I have not written in my journal for almost a month now. Oh, I feel so delinquent, but there hasn't been time. We've been so busy, and if any writing is done, it must first be done for Miss Cunningham, to report events.

I interviewed two women for the job of companion here. The first one I hired had a three-year-old child. It was not a good idea. She had no place to leave the child and so brought her here. We are not equipped for children, I fear, and the child wouldn't let go of her mother's skirts. The mother, a decent enough woman, spent all her time down at the wharf, wading in the water with the little girl. I think, being a widow, she had eyes for Upton. I had to dismiss her.

I hired a second one, who claimed she had a husband out west and no children. Within two days I found my locket missing. Upton missed his pocket watch, and he himself searched her room and found both articles.

She cried, saying she needed money to go out west and join her husband. Upton was very firm. He said he would not tell the authorities if she would go quietly.

She went. I shall not hire any more.

I received a letter from my friend Mary that she can't come for a while. Her mother is not yet well. Upton's aunt Eleanor came to act as chaperone and only upset the whole household. She needed so much special care. I must sit and sew with her every afternoon. I must listen to stories about

Upton and his brothers when they were children.

We must have a formal tea every afternoon, which meant that Upton had to come in from the fields or wherever he was working, change, and wash and dress and sip tea.

She was a dear, but I was glad to see her go.

Of course the servants observed and listened. We have no secrets from them here.

"You let me sleep at the foot of your bed in a cot and you got no need for a chaperone," Priscilla said one day.

We were at supper, which Upton and I take in the dining room every evening. We looked at each other across the table. And I wondered if he felt as foolish as I did.

"That sounds like a fine idea," he said.

After she left the room, I looked at him. "Do you know what you just did to me? I'll have no privacy at all now."

"She can vouch for you if people have anything to say," he said.

"Do I need somebody to vouch for me? Or you?" I asked boldly.

"We both know better than that," he said. And he gave me his smile, which cut into me somehow. I felt a surge in my chest where I suppose my heart is.

I breathed easier. "I'm glad to hear it," I said.

But Priscilla moved her cot into my room anyway, to the foot of my bed. And I have to say that when I awoke the next morning to hear the cannons muttering in the distance, I was glad she was there.

Nine

*I*t was six o'clock in the morning when the cannons mumbled in the distance. And there is no worse sound in the world. It seemed to me that even here, on these placid green lawns, I could feel the earth move.

From that moment until one o'clock in the afternoon, the firing continued in the direction of Centreville.

"Stay calm," Upton told the servants. "No one will come this way."

But they were skittish all day. And for good reason. There didn't seem to be even three minutes' time between each cannon roar. I tried to sew. I tried to pull weeds in my garden, where my peas are already six inches high. In the garden I noticed the birds were lulled into quiet. I looked for my pet crow, but he did not come. Were the animals and birds in hiding?

I tried to write to Miss Cunningham and couldn't. I wanted to pray for the poor souls out there in the distance who had seen their last sunrise that day, and couldn't.

Upton attempted to get the work crew to finish shoring up the pillars on the piazza and to start painting them, but the Nigras couldn't concentrate, so he started them on the road to the general's tomb. It must be repaired.

At one o'clock Priscilla and Jane took the workmen's noon meal out to them, and Upton came into the house and asked for some bread and lemonade and ham. Emily was nowhere to be found. She was hiding somewhere.

I can't say how much safer I felt with just Upton's presence. Then the firing ceased. We looked at each other in the kitchen.

"Regrouping," he said.

Since the other servants were outside, all huddled together in the vicinity of Washington's tomb, I gave him his lunch. He ate morosely.

I knew what was on his mind. "Are you sorry?" I asked.

"About what?"

"That you didn't join the army?"

He nodded his head. "Moments like this, yes."

"You have as much an obligation here, keeping this place from pillage and destruction," I told him.

"I wish I could feel so."

"You know it's true."

"I think the North lost a lot when it lost Lee," he said. It was the only comment he'd said so far about the war.

"What if the North loses?" I asked. "What will become of the country?"

"No matter who loses, it will never be the same," he answered.

Never be the same. He was right. But what would it be?

And why couldn't Mr. Lincoln have offered Lee whatever he wanted to stay? What kind of a president was he? More to the point, what did Lee want? What did any of the South want?

I was sure Upton knew, but I did not ask him.

The cannons stopped for an hour and then recommenced until dark.

The servants and Nigra workmen were not to be found anywhere by the end of the day, so Upton sent the other workmen home. Only Jane came into the kitchen to cook.

The cannons stopped at dusk. The servants came back to the house. Dandridge said a man going by on the river had said that sightseers had been on a hill in Centreville watching the fight. That they ran back to Washington with the retreating Federals, some knocked down and hurt in the melee. That the Federals retreated instead of regrouping, wounded and bloodstained and dying. That the Rebels were headed to Washington City.

But Southern general Beauregard did not follow up and take Washington.

That evening Mrs. Harbinger came around. I let her in the front door. "Oh, thank heavens, Sarah, thank God above. We won a marvelous victory."

"We?" I asked.

"Yes, the South."

I offered to make her tea, but she said she had to go on

and give the news to the neighbors. The Long Bridge had been tied up all day, she said, with wagons carrying the wounded back to Washington. She had heard that thousands were dead.

That night a terrible thing happened. I awoke to hear voices in the near distance. I went to my window and saw torches, the light of which gave me sight of men wandering on the lawns, in and about the trees.

Priscilla stirred in her cot at the foot of my bed. "What be happenin'?"

"Men," I whispered. "Soldiers wandering outside."

We went downstairs, where we met Upton walking about with a candle in hand. He was fully dressed.

"Who are they?" I asked.

"Likely strays from the battle who've wandered over."

"Should we go to them? Do you think they are hurt?"

He handed the candle to me and went to the dining room and came out with his musket. "If they are, it isn't our place to care for them. We haven't the means. Stay right there. Tell the servants to be quiet."

He went to the front windows, but I went too and peered out.

"Put down the candle if you're going to stand here," he whispered fiercely.

I did so.

It seemed like an hour that we stood there watching

those figures wander the lawns with their makeshift torches. To me they looked like ghosts. I thought: *Mayhap they are. Mayhap they've died in the battle and have come to tell General Washington what has happened.*

My thoughts wandered, too, in all directions as we stood there.

Finally the tall case clock behind us in the hall struck the hour. One in the morning. The sliver of moon outside went behind a cloud. It looked like it might rain.

The figures came closer to the piazza.

"I'm going out," Upton said. And he picked up his rifle.

"Oh, please, be careful!" I admonished.

He gave me a look of annoyance, as one of my brothers would, and went out the front door. I saw some other figures come from behind trees and bushes when they saw him. All had torches, and their burning gave a fearful and dreadful light.

I heard Upton talking, heard the men's replies. Was I expected to go out? The presence of a lady here, Miss Cunningham had said, would give the place protection. But Upton would take exception to my presence now. He seemed to be handling things.

The visitors turned to go. He came back inside and locked the door.

"They thought the place was empty," he said. "Likely they wanted to bed down here. They're from a Southern regiment, and they've been in the battle and they seem somewhat dazed."

"Are they going to leave?" I asked.

"They are going to find their way back to their regiment. I gave them directions to where they wanted to go."

He said we should all go to bed then. Priscilla and I went upstairs. But I couldn't sleep. I kept watch, out the windows. It seemed like hours that the men wandered around outside. Their voices carried on the air as they shouted back and forth to one another.

I knew that Upton was downstairs in the foyer with his rifle.

I wanted to go to him. But I also knew, because I had two older brothers, how that would displease him. So I sat on my bed and watched the torchlights going from place to place outside.

At first Priscilla sat up on her bed too. Then she lay down. Then I heard her snoring. It comforted me. And finally, oh, I am so ashamed! I put my head down too and fell asleep.

Ten

*T*he next morning when I awoke, the silence seemed strange. And the wind was blowing from the west. It had rained during the night. The bushes and gardens were still dripping water, and the world seemed washed clean, as if no battle had ever taken place.

"How late were you up?" I asked Upton in the kitchen.

He was finishing his breakfast. Why did I get the feeling he had never gone back to bed? "They meant no harm," he said. "They were simply lost and dazed from the fighting."

He took a final sip of coffee and got up and reached for the musket. "Nevertheless, I'm going to visit the neighbors today to try to start a Home Guard. Dandridge knows what must be done."

He took his horse. Yes, he has a horse. Calls her Peaches. She's a roan color with a light mane. Very pretty. It surprised me somehow, though, seeing him on a horse with a musket. But then, I forget. He is Southern. And it is their men's First Commandment that they learn to shoot and ride. He was morose that morning. I suppose not being in the battle made him morose. I hope he doesn't decide to join.

We still didn't know who had won the battle the day before. And I kept telling myself that to us here at Mount Vernon, it doesn't matter.

Around noontime I was picking some beans in my garden, glad to see my crow back, when I heard the workmen and servants shouting and running beyond the bowling green to the far reaches of the property. I ran to see them pointing at the heavens.

Now what? I thought. *The South's President Jeff Davis on a cloud bank?*

It was a balloon. Nothing less. The servants and workmen alike ran in the direction in which it was coming down, on the edge of our plantation.

I ran too and stood, openmouthed, with the others as the basket, holding a man in a tall black ridiculous hat, hit the ground. Immediately the men grabbed the sides of the skidding basket and brought it to a halt on the road just outside the west gate.

"Thank you, thank you, gentlemen," the man inside said. And he nimbly jumped out, took off his hat, seeing me, and bowed. "I am Professor Thaddeus S. C. Lowe," he said, "special agent of President Abraham Lincoln, commissioned by him to send telegraph messages from the air to the White House. To whom am I speaking?"

I introduced myself.

"Ah, I have heard of the Association and its good ladies. Could I trouble you to let your men help me hide my conveyance here while I telegraph my wife to come and get me?"

"As long as you don't come on our property," I said. "We do not give succor to either side. We are neutral in this war."

"Miss Tracy," he said, "I wish I had the luxury to be neutral, but I do not. How I envy you, yes, how I envy you. That's it, men, gather the balloon in. Be careful there."

He then proceeded to explain its hydrogen-generation apparatus to the men, who were fascinated, all thoughts of mundane work forgotten. They gathered in the colorful folds of the balloon, which now looked like a painted beached whale. He told them what to do and they did it. I stood by, still in amazement. The night before, dazed men with primitive torches, and that morning a balloon! What kind of war was this?

After assuring me that he would not come onto our property, and that he would send our workers home soon, Mr. Lowe said his wife would be coming in a covered wagon, disguised as a farm woman, to take him back to Washington.

What had he seen from the air? one of the men asked him.

He could not say. It was military intelligence. He was working for President Lincoln. He was scouting the placement of Southern troops.

He said the North lost the battle the day before, and that if Southern general Beauregard had the sense of a mountain goat (which he doesn't), he could have followed his win up with taking Washington. He said that before the battle the soldiers in Washington City were getting rowdy and drunk. He said the best possible order did not prevail in Washington but that the town was a great, confused garrison.

"But the North has had its first defeat," he said, "and no one is very happy."

Upton succeeded in getting enough men for a Home Guard.

He told me the Confederates have declared July 30 to be a muster day. And that many men in the area who do not wish to be drafted into the Southern army will be making their way North. "Don't let any of them in if they come this way and you want to be considered neutral," he told me.

I said I would be careful.

This afternoon some soldiers came by to see the house and Washington's tomb. We made $7.25 from them. We are in need of money. I decided to send Dandridge to Alexandria with another load of cabbages to sell.

On muster day a group of Northern officers came by. We greeted them, and I showed them the tomb. They adhered to my rules as to covering their signs of rank on their uniforms and setting their guns down. But then I got the feeling that, being officers, they wanted to be invited to dinner.

I had just shown them the house when the smell of

cooking wafted in from the kitchen. They lingered.

"Gentlemen, I would invite you, but I am under command also," I said, "to stay neutral and not show favor in this war. I know the people at Hollin Hall are prepared today for visitors," I told them. "They are just half a mile from here." I gave them directions.

As luck would have it, Upton was not with us. He was out amongst the neighbors, vouching for those who had joined his Home Guard with the muster men from both North and South. For the North had decided to compete and send men into the area also, to recruit.

I was just sitting down in the dining room by myself when there came a knock on our front door. *More officers*, I thought. But it wasn't.

It was Robert Harbinger. "Miss Tracy, can I please come in?"

He had a blanket strapped onto his back, army fashion. "Are you here for something for your mother?" I asked.

"No. I'm hiding from my mother. I'll explain if you let me in."

I know I shouldn't have, but I did. After all, I'm hiding from my mother too, aren't I? He stepped into the foyer. "I want to join the Northern army," he said. "Today. And I know my mother won't let me. So I've come here to hide until I see a muster man from the North."

"But I can't hide a soldier," I said. "You know how I'm supposed to stay neutral."

"I'm not a soldier. Not yet. Miss Tracy, I'm sure a Northern recruiter will be by soon. I just ask you to let me stand here and peek out the windows until I see one. Then I'll go. I promise."

I let him stay. I know I shouldn't have. And soon a recruiter was sighted, across the bowling green in back, on the other side of our fence.

"He's Northern!" Robert was ecstatic. "The man is from the North! He's wearing a blue uniform. I'm going, Miss Tracy. And I thank you."

"Just like that?" I stared at him. "You're going to war?"

"Yes. It's the only way. Otherwise my mother will stop me."

And he went out the back door. I watched him stride masterfully across the bowling green in back and hail the recruiter. I watched them speak awhile. I saw him hand the recruiter a paper. And then they turned and walked back to the fence. And to the road that took them away from Mount Vernon.

Well, General Washington, I thought, *I know how badly you need men. You've got one more now. God bless him.*

Eleven

So now I am deemed a spy.

This time it is a Philadelphia newspaper. They suggest I am "residing at Mount Vernon and entertaining friends there like a princess."

Like a princess, yes, especially when I help Upton scrape the wallpaper off the dining-room walls in its refurbishing. More especially when I weed my garden. Maybe somebody saw me talking to my pet crow and decided he was a member of my court.

These same troublemakers say that Mount Vernon has been paid for by Northern money and that I now make frequent trips from here to Washington to "damage the free states and assist the armed traitors in the South."

Why must people be such meddlesome troublemakers? Don't they know that if you leave trouble alone, it will find you?

The article went on to say that I was seen talking to Professor Thaddeus Lowe in the field, "gathering information to give to the Southern traitors."

Whatever else they say of me, *I will not be construed as a spy!* I must write, today, to all the Northern vice-regents and to Miss Cunningham to have them respond to these falsehoods.

But what hurts even more in the article is that it claims that *we employ slave labor here at Mount Vernon.*

It says our Nigras are not paid. That they are not free.

Upton advises we don't respond to any of it. Isn't that just like a man? My brothers would say the same thing. But I cannot abide such lies, when we are all working so hard to put this place to rights.

"We must free the Nigras," I told him.

He sighed. He scratched his head. He rubbed the bridge of his nose. "Do you know how to do this?" he asked.

I was dumbfounded. The how of it had never occurred to me.

I didn't know how. And it came to me, for all my family's abolitionist talk up North, that I never have known how. I thought for a moment.

"I would think something like this should be done by President Lincoln," he said.

"Well, he isn't here," I said sharply. "And he isn't likely to come."

Upton looked abashed. "Are there some kind of magic words that one says?" he asked. "Some ceremony?"

And then I came to my senses.

"I suppose it is sufficient to gather them together and tell them all that they are now free and may go and do as they please. Those words are magic in themselves. Aren't those the words so many Nigras in the South are praying to hear?"

"And suppose they do just that? Go and do as they please? What will we do without them?"

"Hire others! What is it about you Southerners that you think you can't do without your Nigras?"

He took the scolding in good cheer. "Who will make my mint julep if Jane goes?"

"Stop joking. We must do it. This very day."

And then he had a thought. "I think it involves free papers. I think that I'll have to write it out and file it at the courthouse. Now that I think of it, my father did that once for one of his slaves when I was a child."

"All right," I said. "Then, you must do it."

So this very day we gathered them on the piazza, and Upton told them that they were free. They could leave us if they wished. They no longer had to stay in our employ. In his hands he had papers he had written out for each of them. He told them always to keep a copy and that another would be filed at the Fairfax County Courthouse for them as soon as possible.

Jane shook her head as if we were pure mad. Emily nudged Priscilla. "You do this?" I heard her whisper savagely. "You do this jus' to get me to leave?"

Priscilla scowled back.

Dandridge shuffled his feet. "You want me to leave, boss?" he asked Upton.

"Of course not," Upton said.

"Then, why you do this for?"

"I have to do it. The newspapers are saying you're in slavery. It doesn't look good for Miss Tracy."

"We ain't in no slavery," Priscilla mumbled. "If'n I was, an' wanted to be free, doan you think I cudda walked off any time I went travelin' with Miss Sarah?"

We all stood looking at one another, alternately embarrassed and proud. They of their loyalty, and we that we were setting them free.

"Well, at any rate," Upton said, "if anybody asks you, you're free. Now that your papers are in good order."

They walked away mumbling and questioning the sanity of white people.

"We knows we free," I heard Dandridge say to the others.

"They gots to make it look good for themselves," Priscilla answered.

"I cudda run a hunnert times," Emily said. "If I felt like it."

In the evening, when all the chores are done, I often take tea on the piazza. I have managed to convince Upton to sit with me. It is still in disrepair, but at least the falling-down pillars are fixed.

I am told that General Washington and Martha took tea here, though I do not know the exact spot. I am told that

General Washington sat here with General Lafayette, too, and discussed slavery.

When the shadows lengthen, I can believe it. I can believe anything about this place. Things change with the deepening light. In the distance we can hear the frogs croaking on the riverbanks. Tree branches sway in the evening breeze, revealing long-held secrets. But what? I can smell the roses I planted in my flower garden, as well as the geraniums and phlox, mixed with the smell of fresh wood that is lying around for repairs.

I love the smell of fresh wood almost as much as flowers.

The pansies are in borders in the shade because they cannot take full sun. Next to my flower garden is the old greenhouse that George Washington had built so long ago. It burned years ago, and what is left is covered with vines. Vinca grows in a riot of green all around the ground near the mansion. There are wild grapevines down by the river. In the evening, just for a moment or so, I can feel the peace of this place and the secret it is trying to tell me.

All will be well. All will be in order again. What you are doing here is for future generations.

I can pretend the place is not in disarray but will soon be as Washington kept it in its prime. And I can pretend that there is no war.

The letters from the Northern vice-regents went to the papers, including the *Star* in Washington, speaking for my loyalty to the Union and to the slavery question on Mount Vernon.

Things settled down for two days. And then I had a visit from Mrs. Harbinger.

She came driving her own cart one morning, bearing strawberry preserves.

"Have you seen my boy?" she asked. "Has Robert been about?"

I told her no, I hadn't seen him. But it turned out she knew better.

"He was here. I saw him come off your land with that recruiting man. I always knew you were a traitor," she said.

Her words were like a slap. Was she the person who had told the papers about me? That our people were slaves? That I was seen talking to Professor Lowe?

"Mrs. Harbinger," I said sternly, "mind yourself. Those are strong words."

"I don't mind him going," she said. "I have no illusions but that they'll come round for him sooner or later. But to think he joined the Northern army! You are a traitor to have set this up for him. We are Southerners. My other boy died fighting for the South!"

"Your boy died when he fell from a horse," I said.

But she would not hear of it. She sat at the kitchen table and cried. Not because Robert had joined the army. But because he had joined the Northern army.

And somehow I managed to console her, angry as I was.

Because she was confused. But who amongst us isn't these days? I had heard that some of the Quaker neighbors around us were not speaking to one another anymore because one had a son fighting for the North and another for the South.

Don't they have enough confusion making the decision to fight? I thought.

I ended up comforting Mrs. Harbinger. And I served her strawberry preserves.

It is the fifteenth of August. The fixing of the house goes on. The wharf is repaired. Mrs. Frobel was here this morning and told me that when Mrs. Lee left Arlington, she left with a large farm wagon full of good furniture, portraits, china, and furbelows that once belonged to George and Martha Washington. I wish she had put them here for safekeeping. We need furnishings so. The house is so bare that sometimes it echoes.

But no. Mrs. Lee took that wagonload of treasures deeper into Virginia. I hope they survive the war.

Today I heard officially that both of Upton's brothers, Arthur and William, and all his cousins joined the Confederate army. Arthur owns the bank in Alexandria. I heard this from Dandridge.

Mary McMakin says mayhap she can come in September. I think she is fearful of travel. I think she is fearful of being here. She was always afraid of everything. I suppose I should write to her again and tell her I need her to come. At least it will keep Fanny happy.

We heard guns in the distance yesterday. The shots rang out and carried in the air. They seemed not far away, and Upton ordered all the servants and workmen to stay close to the house.

He rode out on Peaches to find the source of the trouble. Turns out it was a skirmish. The redbrick church, where General Washington and his family went, is six miles from here. Upton reports it was not damaged but it was pillaged. Everything inside that could be carried away was taken, even the white baptismal font.

It is this part of war that bothers me so. That baptismal font was an original to the church. What will a soldier do with it?

Mary writes that she is coming in September. Oh, my heart is glad. Not because I fear being the only white woman in the house. But because now speculation about my being alone here with Upton will end.

I am preparing one of the upstairs rooms for Mary.

I have to go to Washington City again. Not only do we need candles and oil, but we need new passes. President Lincoln has put General McClellan in charge, and the pass from General Scott is no longer valid. And our servants need passes to Alexandria. With McClellan, there are all new rules. They say he is pompous and orderly and crazy for regulations.

I must get a new pass even for myself to go to Alexandria. As it is now, we've had mail only once in ten days. And I must have it three times a week or go mad. If only because I must keep up with the papers and see what people are saying about us.

But now we have news of a different stripe. George Washington Riggs is an important banker and treasurer of the Association, and he and his wife have proved good friends. They live two miles short of Alexandria. She writes that Prince Napoléon of France is visiting Washington and wants to visit Mount Vernon.

A prince! Well, we've had just about everything else happen to us. Why not this?

Twelve

*I*n the weeks that followed I tried to remember if there was anything in any of Miss Semple's teachings that prepared one for entertaining a French prince.

There was.

Girls, face your problems. Meet them head-on!

So much had to be done. The workmen were still fixing the road to the west gate. It was filled with ruts from frozen spring mud, which were deep and were now dust beds.

Upton asked me what I wanted done outside. "The hedges must be trimmed," I said, "and the grass around the brick walks. And the walks weeded."

He set the men working.

I had Priscilla bake a cake. Martha Washington's "great cake," for which we had the recipe. I sent for claret and groceries from Alexandria. They would not require supper, we were told. Just refreshment.

And then I had a thought. Did they speak English? Could I remember my French from my days in New Orleans? I have been practicing.

Thank heaven the place speaks for itself. The trees are lush, the lawns green, and the flowers in full bloom.

Though it is August, we have plenty of flowers—lavender, heliotrope, pinks, phlox, ragged robin, Canterbury bell, musk roses, columbine, and sweet William. Even the old orange trees in the middle of the tumbledown greenhouses are in bloom.

I have picked some flowers and put them in vases in the house.

There is a special vase of musk roses in General Washington's bedroom.

Well, the place is ready. We await the prince.

And then came a special messenger, up the road on horseback. I felt myself shake all over. Only bad news comes on horseback.

Upton met him, gave him some money, had the servants give him refreshment, and brought the letter to me.

It was addressed to me.

It was from an officer on Lee's staff.

I looked at Upton. "I don't know if I should open it. I might be accused of consorting with the enemy."

His brown eyes sought mine in understanding, and he held out his hand for the letter, which I gave over.

I watched his expression turn into a scowl. "John Augustine Washington has been killed," he said softly.

"Killed?"

"In the war."

"I didn't know he'd joined up."

"Oh yes, I did. And apparently there was a skirmish in the western part of Virginia. And he was mortally wounded."

I put my hands over my mouth to still the cry. Upton put a hand on my shoulder.

"A man with six children had no right to join the army," I said.

"No, but he had to prove himself."

I thought of him, how he'd been that last morning he was here, when I made him leave the house, how downtrodden and humble. I thought of him dead now. Oh, why had I been so pompous! Because I'd wanted to show my mettle to Upton and Miss Cunningham. And I'd made that poor man my victim. I was so ashamed of myself. Of course he'd gone and joined the army. Mayhap to prove himself to me, how did I know?

I wanted the letter, but I did not take it. I would not let it be said that I had touched a letter from Lee's staff. "Keep it," I told Upton. "You keep it."

He folded it carefully. "I will." His brow was furrowed, his manner solemn.

"Upton, I know what you're thinking," I said. "Don't think it, please."

He shoved his hands into his pockets. "He went and did his duty. And I'm here."

"You're doing your duty," I reminded him.

"What? Entertaining a French prince?"

"No," I said, and my voice was full of resolve. "Keeping General Washington's house from being pillaged and destroyed. Look what happened to Pohick Church. What will future generations have, if not for what you're doing?"

"It's you who are doing it," he mumbled. And he walked away, toward the old slave quarters, which I dearly wished had been taken down, but which, to this day, haven't.

I was about to go after him when somebody yelled that there was a carriage coming up the road to the house.

I ran up to my room to change. I put on my best print dress and was fixing my hair. I knew I must greet them. Upton was likely walking in the road near the slave quarters, sulking. He often walks there when he wants to be alone.

Then I heard voices and looked out my window. It was Upton and several men, walking about. He was showing them the gardens, and they were responding in *French*.

I ran downstairs and outside to see Upton escorting them to the tomb. Good, that would give me more time. I must make lemonade. I went into the pantry to mix it, then needed the punch bowl from the sideboard in the dining room, so I went to fetch it.

There I ran into two of them.

I was startled, but I curtsied. So they bowed. Then I said something, in French, about the heat. Their eyes went wide that I could speak the language, and I invited them into the kitchen for a glass of lemonade.

There we sat at the table. They were two aides, and there were seven in their party—the prince, who they called Plon-Plon, five aides, and Count Mercier.

I showed these two aides Lafayette's room. I let them handle the key to the Bastille. All the while I was watching Upton, hoping the news of John Augustine Washington wouldn't put a damper on him.

If it did, they didn't notice. Upton was the perfect Southern gentleman. He told them all about the house, its history, its problems now. I interpreted for the others, but the prince spoke English.

They nodded and smiled. Then they told us their problems.

They'd had no breakfast. Their driver didn't know the roads. Their horses were not up to the job, and they were anxious to have them cared for and find others. They needed to get back to Washington, but if they couldn't change horses, they needed a village hotel on the way.

At once I ordered a late breakfast be cooked up. Jane went right to it. I served them claret. I supervised in the kitchen while Upton entertained them in the dining room.

We cooked everything we had.

The prince was a quiet man of pleasant features and impeccable manners. He told us he was the son of Jérôme Bonaparte, that his wife was an Italian princess who was now visiting in New York, and that he was not welcome in the court of his cousin Napoléon III. "So I travel," he said.

He described, briefly, his travels. "We dined with Mr. Lincoln and saw the Federal encampments around Washington. Then," the prince said, "with a flag of truce, we went from McClellan's headquarters at Arlington to Jeb Stuart at the Fairfax courthouse. Ah, but when we came out of the woods and we saw this house," he said. "To think of this house, where the famous general once lived, standing so upright in the middle of all the chaos, like a white dream."

A white dream. I had never thought of it that way.

"The spirit of war is so near, yet this little corner of the world is so quiet, so safe," he went on, "sacred ground. It is a fact, in itself, in the history of the world, what this house stands for," he said. "And it is my fervent hope that you may keep it this way."

They stayed until four o'clock. I told them of Washington and the Marquis de Lafayette walking the grounds here, how the Frenchman had been like a son to Washington during the war. I told them of the visit of the duke of Orléans in 1797, before he became King Louis Philippe.

They were introduced to the servants. They tipped them for their service.

"We are descended from George Washington's slaves," Priscilla told them.

Before they left, I got a small box, filled it with soil and small rare plants from near the tomb, and placed it in their carriage. And when the prince and his party left, they were going back to Washington pulled by two Mount Vernon mules.

I thought that mayhap the visit would restore Upton's spirits. But he was once again morose when they left. He walked out alone, smoking a cheroot. I saw the tip of it glowing in the dark off a ways from the piazza.

Oh, I hope he does not decide to join the army! I hope we do not lose him. Must I worry about that now too?

My sister, Fanny, has written again. To me. She says she has heard from Mary McMakin that she is not here with me but still in Philadelphia. She asks what woman is here with me. And if there is none, she will come, war or no war.

"I hope you are not there alone with Mr. Herbert," she writes. "Do you realize what a disgrace that will be on the family if you are found out?"

Disgrace, indeed. Her accusation brought tears to my eyes, especially when I looked at Upton. Why, he is the dearest, kindest, most honorable man I have ever met.

He would die before he disgraced me. And I mustn't let him know what she has written, or he might join the army just to save my reputation.

I found myself hoping that if Fanny took it upon herself to come here, she would get snared in one of the Union army blockades. Or captured by Confederate cavalryman Jeb Stuart.

I have written again to Mary asking her, for heaven's sake, to come. I will get her a special pass from Mr. Lincoln if necessary. "If you don't come, you sentence me to my sister, Fanny," I have written.

Today I had Dandridge harness the mules to the wagon, and I drove the fifteen miles to Washington like a farm woman, with a load of cabbages to sell. Upton didn't want me to go. "I'm safer than you would be," I told him. "And I need to get a pass from McClellan for Mary McMakin."

What a day! First I disposed of all the cabbages at the Washington market. Then I purchased some salt and pepper and much-needed coffee and sugar for us. On to McClellan's headquarters at Arlington, where I had to run several gauntlets of pickets to get through.

I had never been in Lee's home before and was looking forward to it. But I soon found that McClellan was at his other office in town and that his assistant could write me a pass if I wanted. I very much wanted. But it was done quickly, outside the house in a tent. So I never got inside. Well, at least I got the pass for Mary, and new ones for myself and the servants, too, since General Scott's don't do the job anymore. Arlington seems very bare, not only of decorations, but of essentials to such a magnificent home.

I have to admit that I lingered too long, looking longingly at the outside of the house, taking my time driving the buggy on the grounds. Darkness near overtook me on the ride home. I had to watch for the many roadblocks set up against Confederate raiders and show my own pass at each one.

Some of the Union pickets were nice. Others were snide, and all I could hope was that some ambitious one wouldn't shoot me first and ask questions later.

When I got home, I expected Upton to scold, but he couldn't. We had a visitor, a man named Winslow Homer, who is an artist working for *Harper's* magazine and is on his way to join the Federal army and do some sketches.

Upton was entertaining him in the parlor. They were drinking claret, and Mr. Homer was talking about the importance of clean outlines on his engravings. Upton introduced me. I asked him if he was staying the night. He said Upton had prepared a room for him. So I went directly to bed.

Mr. Homer stayed two days and he worked the whole time. He set up his easel and drew a pencil sketch of the mansion from the side. On leaving he gave it to me.

"Upton tells me you need money here," he said.

I would not have spoken to him of money. Only a man could do that. But I said, "Yes, we do. We have a budget. The roof needs repairing, and that will cost at least a hundred dollars."

"You may have copies of the sketch made and sell them, if it helps," he suggested.

I looked up at him. He was famous. He had spent a year in France. He was a regular contributor to *Harper's Weekly*. He was a tall, rangy man with the saddest eyes I had ever seen.

"Thank you," I said. "Mayhap we will do that."

"This place is in good hands," he said. "If I had time, I'd do more. There are dramatic contrasts of light and dark. Perhaps I'll stop back again sometime."

"Please do, Mr. Homer."

He left the next morning before I was downstairs. *Yes, Mr. Homer,* I thought, *there are dramatic contrasts of light and dark. Did you see it as I do? The light is so clean, with such dramatic, certain lines. And the dark is so troubled and fearful.*

I am keeping the sketch in my room. Someday we may need to copy and sell it.

Thirteen

We have a pass for Dandridge, the one I got when I went to Arlington. It says: "Pass Dandridge Smith (colored) with wagon, mules, and provisions, for the Mount Vernon Association in and out of Washington and Alexandria when necessary."

It is signed by General McClellan's assistant.

The first time Dandridge used it, it worked. The second time, it didn't. I had to go to Alexandria myself to get the mail. And I was stopped several times and didn't think I'd get through.

"Better you get passes from the general himself," one officer told me.

I prepared to go to McClellan's office again to find out what had happened. Of course Upton didn't want me going alone and made me take Priscilla.

For two miles outside Alexandria we ran into nothing but soldiers and camps, heard nothing but shouts and martial music. I used to love the sound of a fife and a drum. I hate it now. And oh, how I hate military uniforms!

I didn't know which of his offices McClellan would be at, so we first went to Arlington. Of course we had to pass through about six picket points and have our passes checked. Every second lieutenant, it seemed, must have his say. Then to McClellan's office. This time, it turned out, he was there. So I was ushered inside Lee's great house.

They made Priscilla wait outside. Inside they made me wait an hour. I sat there in the hall staring at the blank spots on the walls, which were cleaner than the rest of the paper because family portraits had once hung there. I wondered whose portraits they were, if any of them had been of Nelly Custis, Washington's granddaughter, and where they had ended up.

Aides were walking around with cups of coffee. Do you think they would offer me one? The smell drove me wild.

I had heard about McClellan. He was no more than thirty-five, yet was in charge of 300,000 men. He considered himself the nation's savior. He was guarded wherever he went by an escort of dragoons. He called his horse Dan Webster. Every layabout and vagabond had disappeared from Washington's streets since his arrival or had rushed across Rock Creek to avoid arrest.

He brought order of one kind and chaos of another. The chaos of military occupation. Wine, brandy, and bourbon seized at the Long Bridge ended up in the flour sacks and pickle barrels of the military. Because of his influence Congress created the Metropolitan Police.

Finally I was admitted into the pompous man's office.

"Ah, Miss Tracy," he said. And he stood there looking more like Napoléon than Prince Napoléon had. His uniform was plain blue without shoulder straps. He sported a red mustache. On his head he wore a French kepi. "How can I help you today?"

"The passes your assistant gave my servants and myself have no value," I said. "I need new ones."

"My assistant never wrote passes for your servants," he said.

Did I dare show him the pass for Dandridge? I did. "It looks like a forgery," he said.

"Your aide wrote it."

"Well, he had no right to. I would not write such passes."

"Then, how are we supposed to get about?"

"I cannot write passes for every servant and young girl in Fairfax County," he said. "The result would be chaos. Servants cannot be trusted."

I wanted to say that we had chaos now. I was so angry. I could not prove his aide had written my passes, because I'd not been in the tent at the time. But I was sure he had. "Will you write me one, then? I need to get to Alexandria. And Washington. For food. We're running out of necessities at home, and the workmen must be fed."

"Young girls such as yourself should stay off the roads," he said. And he would not be moved.

I did not want to beg. But I begged. For Mount Vernon.

Until finally he held up his hand and said, "Then, perhaps a higher authority."

"What authority?" I asked.

"President Lincoln," he said. And he smiled, sneakily and with satisfaction.

"Now, if you will excuse me, I must get to my headquarters. My wife and baby girl are joining me today."

I blinked. "I thought this was your headquarters."

"I spend twelve to fourteen hours a day on horseback, Miss Tracy. My headquarters is on H Street near Lafayette Park."

I left in a rage. He darned well could have written me another pass. The little toad!

"You'd best get another pass, miss," one of his aides who'd overheard the conversation told me on the way out. "Federal pickets are moving within three miles of Mount Vernon."

All around the city soldiers were building earthworks, on both sides of the river. I could see that it was ruining the farmers' land. Their orchards and gardens were filled with tents. Their trees and fences were being cut down. Their cattle displaced, their soil transformed into high piles of dirt and deep ditches. We would have famine this winter for the sake of earthworks.

I knew better than to go first to President Lincoln. So I went to General Scott. At least he had treated me decently the last time we met, even though his passes had been overridden by McClellan.

Under McClellan's new regulations certainly Scott's name would be good on passes this time, wouldn't it?

I got to the War Department building and left Priscilla in the carriage with instructions not to move the wagon. "I am on important business with General Scott," I told her. And I left her a note with my name on it and the name of the Association.

Inside was the usual crowd of hangers-on, favor seekers, and soldiers. I pushed my way through to General Scott's aide and told him what I wanted.

"He isn't in today, miss. He's sick."

"Then, who do I see?"

He shrugged. "The president. Lincoln. If McClellan has refused you, there is no power on Earth who can help you now but President Lincoln."

"How do I do that?" I asked.

He said to go right to the White House. He grinned. "Everybody else does," he told me.

So, on to the White House. And more maneuvering to find a place for our buggy, and the same instructions to Priscilla. All I managed to absorb, as I was led by a soldier through the president's house, was a glimpse of the Blue Room and the elegant carpets underfoot.

I was in the White House! What would Fanny say? I

wondered as I climbed the stairs to the president's office. Would she still insist on coming to fetch me home?

Likely she'd scold me at this moment because my dress wasn't fancy enough or my shoes dusty.

What would Miss Semple think of me now?

When I finally got in to see him, the president was at the window in his office, reading something. His glasses were on the edge of his nose. He was dressed in black, as I expected. But he appeared rumpled, from his cravat to his wrinkled trousers.

"Miss Sarah Tracy, sir, from the Mount Vernon Ladies' Association," his secretary announced me.

Would he remonstrate with me for not receiving his wife that day? Would he even know of it?

"Ah." He turned, adjusted his spectacles, and looked at me. "Do sit, Miss Tracy. Can you believe that I do not have a telegraph in my office? That I must go over to the War Department and Mr. Stanton's office to get news?"

I nodded and smiled. He didn't have scores of guards, like McClellan had. Or an expensive uniform. Or more than one headquarters.

A servant came in, peered at a plate of food on his desk. "Mr. President, sir, you haven't eaten," he said sadly.

"Food does not appeal to me, Henley. Get me an apple."

The servant took the plate and left. Mr. Lincoln sat. His bony knees stuck out in front. He didn't seem to know what to do with his hands. He was all arms and legs. His face was sallow and wrinkled, but when he smiled and asked me about how Mount Vernon was doing, I felt a whole sense of warmth, I felt the world opening up for me, and I found myself telling him my troubles.

"I must come to see you there sometime," he said. "I must come and see the general's tomb."

The servant returned with an apple on a plate. Mr. Lincoln proceeded to pick it up and peel it with a knife, trying to get all the skin off in one long peel.

"Can you do this, Miss Tracy?" he asked.

"I did it once, sir," I said.

"It's an accomplishment," he said. "Go on, so you were saying that General McClellan denied his aide's issuing your passes."

"I'm sure he forgot, sir. He has many responsibilities."

"Yes, I'm sure." Then he smiled, and the homely face was full of a sort of rapture. "Like the farmer said to the pig after he slit its throat, Miss Tracy: 'You must forgive me. I forgot you were the one I was going to let live. Next time I'll do better.'"

We laughed at the joke together, and when he laughed, he hee-hee-heed and slapped his knee. The apple was peeled. The peeling was all of a piece.

"May I offer you a piece of apple?"

"No, sir, thank you. But you eat, you must be hungry."

"I'm never hungry. But I'll eat when you leave. First let

me give you a letter for General McClellan. He'll sign your passes, I promise you."

He scribbled out a letter. "My secretary, Mr. Hay, is swamped with work." And I thought, *Even Miss Cunningham wouldn't write her own letters.*

I thanked him profusely, and he stood, a tall, gangling man who did not look polished and elegant like McClellan, but who did look as if he knew what the war was all about.

"It's been my pleasure, Miss Tracy. Take care of the general's home for us. One of these days maybe I'll have the time to visit."

He took my hand, not to kiss, but to shake, vigorously. And it was over.

I found my way back downstairs. As I left the room I heard him munching the apple.

Over to H Street then, where McClellan said he would be, near Lafayette Park. Government wagons raised dust in the street. The sun was getting hot. I longed for something cool to drink. Or some of that apple the president was eating when I left.

"How was the president?" Priscilla asked me.

"Wonderful," I told her, "just as we've been told he is. A real *person*."

"You think he be as good as Washington?"

I was surprised at the question. And even more surprised at my answer. "He is what we need right now, as

Washington was what we needed then," I told her. And she nodded and understood.

Of course there were sentries, twelve of them, in front of McClellan's fancy brick house. Of course the house had wrought-iron gates and flowers in front, and long ceiling-to-floor windows and marble floors inside.

Of course I had to wait again and sit and watch the aides and officers running in and out with the purpose of such importance that I felt part of the wall when they passed.

And of course McClellan was annoyed when he looked up from his desk to see me again.

"I told you to go to the president," he said, as if speaking to a stubborn child.

"I did," I said. "He gave me this for you." And I handed him the letter. It had been sealed by the president, of course, so I do not know what was in it, but whatever was in it made General George McClellan's face redden.

"I never told you my aide didn't write the passes," he said. "Of course he wrote the passes. What I told you was that he had no right to do so. And regulations have changed since then. But of course, Miss Tracy, I will write new ones."

The voice softened until it became like syrup. "It's just all a grand mistake," he said. "And I will do anything in the world I can to help you." He wrote quickly. I asked for a pass for Mary McMakin, and he wrote that, too.

"I'll send a steam tug with provisions to Mount Vernon

if you need it. All you have to do is ask, Miss Tracy."

So, I thought when I left. *So. One has all the guards of the queen of England, and the spit-and-polish uniform and the fancy furbelows of rank and privilege. The other peels his own apples and doesn't even have a telegraph in his office. I didn't see an officer in sight. And yet this one cowers before the words of the other.*

I don't think General McClellan will last long, I told myself, going back outside. *I don't think so at all.*

Priscilla and I got some frozen ices from a street vendor. Then some hot pretzels and coffee. Then we went to the Washington market to shop for meat and vegetables and other items.

The new passes worked wonders on the ride home.

Fourteen

Mary is here. I made another trip to Washington to bring her. She is at once fearful of the war and animated because of all the soldiers. Every time we were stopped at a picket point, I noticed her fluttering her eyelashes at the sentries. Oh well, this is an adventure for her. She has led a sheltered life.

The heat of the summer has abated somewhat with the onset of September. Mary likes her room, but I fear she does not like Upton. "Does he have to be here all the time?" she asked me. "Even when we eat?"

"He lives here," I told her.

"With you?" And she giggled.

"Mary, it isn't like that," I told her. "He is the dearest man. I could not do this without him."

"Are you in love with him, then?"

"But of course not."

"Then, you shouldn't call him dearest."

"Well, I don't say it to his face, of course!"

It is as if we are back at Troy Female Seminary again, where Mary was my roommate. Back then we told each other everything. But that was a hundred years ago. Only Mary, with her pert little-girl ways, is still back there, and I am not.

"Do you remember?" she will say. "Alice Charles? And the time we picked the apples in the orchard when we were forbidden to? The farmer stormed right into the school building and told Miss Semple to keep her hussies off his land. Do you remember?"

And she goes on and on.

She chats constantly. While all this is going on, of course, Upton is at the table too, trying to read his paper. Usually he will read it of a morning at breakfast and tell me the news. Now he just reads it solemnly.

They do not get on. Right from the minute they met, there was animosity. And after just two days they were fighting openly.

"I think you are rude to read the paper while we are talking," Mary told him the second morning at breakfast.

Upton had never been called rude in his life. He was taken aback. "I thought you two were having a private conversation," he said.

"We want to include you," Mary told him.

"It's rude to speak of things in front of a third person of which that person knows nothing," he chided.

"Oh, excuse me, the Southern gentleman is holding forth!" Mary said with exaggerated politeness.

"Stop it, you two. This will never do. We have to live here together!"

But Mary would not stop it. And polite and imbued with

Southern grace as he is, Upton took exception to her snip-
ing, for which I did not blame him.

I don't know what I shall do with the both of them. It is
as if the war between the North and the South has come
into our kitchen.

Mary is small and fair and very pretty and fragile looking, but that look is deceiving. She is iron willed. As the
only daughter of an indulgent father, she has been
taught to stand on her own, yes, to speak out, yes, but
the trouble is that the part of her that will always be a
girl sometimes wins over the part of her that learned to
be a woman.

She has terrible vanity, and everything must always be
about her. I thought, being a Southern man, Upton would
recognize those qualities. But I think he does not like
them.

Still, I think he could try harder. And I am getting
annoyed with both of them already.

A good thing and a bad thing happened on this beautiful
September day. Upton's brothers, Arthur and William,
came by in their Confederate uniforms to say good-bye
before they went off to war.

Upton was repairing the roof with the workmen. I get so
frightened when he gets up there on the roof. I hear the

hammering inside the house, and it seems to shake every-thing, including me. And then I think as long as we have hammering, it means he hasn't fallen off.

I dread his falling off. We are nowhere near any help if anything happened to him or one of the workmen.

He got down immediately when his brothers came, of course, and I was surprised to see them hug. Upton called a stop to the work, and the workmen had lemonade while he brought his brothers into the house.

"We've been here before," Arthur said. "When we helped Upton move in his belongings."

We sat at the dining-room table, and Jane gave us coffee and some fresh buns. I could not but notice two things about the visit. For one, Upton looked with such envy on the uniforms his brothers wore that it broke my heart. For another, Mary looked with such flirtatious eyes at them it embarrassed me. And I think it embarrassed them, too.

When it came time to say good-bye, I wished them luck and all but dragged Mary into the house so Upton could have a quiet moment with his brothers.

They do look dashing in their officer's uniforms with the swords at their sides. Their horses are sleek and noble looking. They are, of course, both cavalry. And my heart leaped in my breast as they rode away and I saw Upton, his workman's hat in his hand, watching them go.

To think that they are off to fight, and mayhap kill some Northern boy I might know, devastates me.

A wonderful thing has happened to smooth out the tension in this house now. Miss Cunningham wrote to me from South Carolina and said she has acquired the English harpsichord that belonged to Nelly Custis. Despite the war, it is being shipped north and will come by boat up the river.

We have heard that the army is going to confiscate our own boat for the use of troops. Oh, I hope the harpsichord gets here safely. She said I was to write to her the minute it came.

As part of the fall harvest I have the servants picking apples. I intend to make applesauce and preserve it for the winter months. I cannot, however, enlist Mary. She refuses to do any work but embroidery.

She is making an altar cloth for the church she attended in Philadelphia. It is very long and of white linen, and she is embroidering angels and cherubs and just about every vision of heaven on it.

I think it is useless right now, when we must not only harvest the food, but put it away for winter. But then, I must be fair. I did not ask Mary here to do servants' work. I asked her to be my companion only, and she expected no more from the job.

I was right. Upton is even more cast down now since the visit of his brothers. He is quieter than ever, though still polite and courtly to Mary, who I think drives him crazy.

We have a note about the harpsichord! It will arrive tomorrow by boat! Oh, I hope the weather holds! Oh, where shall we put it? I think in the Little Parlor, the room where we sometimes receive visitors.

I have been reading some about Nelly Custis. She was Martha's granddaughter, and the general loved her so! She was married to Lawrence Lewis, his nephew, on the general's last birthday, in February of 1799. He never had another birthday. He died before the year ended.

And oh, it must be some kind of a sign! This book says Nelly loved to play the harpsichord for the general in the Little Parlor. Exactly where I have decided to put it.

Sometimes I feel so close to General Washington in this house that it is eerie. But then, I walk in his footsteps. I sit where he sat. I gaze at what he gazed at outside. How can one not feel his spirit? I wonder if Upton ever does. I must ask him.

The harpsichord has come, wrapped in blankets, guarded by bales of hay, and undamaged. Upton had all the men go to the wharf to get it off the boat. He had it put on a wagon pulled by mules up to the house. It was a tedious business, for he insisted the mules go very slow.

Then he himself chose the workmen who would carry it into the Little Parlor. They were very careful, as if it were a priceless vase, only bigger.

Then I polished it carefully.

"May I play?" Mary asked when I was finished.

Upton knows I play. He wiped his hands with a rag and just stood there. I felt it was pushy of Mary. Miss Semple would be ashamed of her. But she seems to have no shame. "Of course," I said. And she sat right down and played "Home, Sweet Home."

The strains of that song always tug at my heartstrings. I thought of Mother and Father and my own home up in Troy, which I hadn't seen in a few years now. And I was determined to do better than ever here, in this home entrusted to my care.

I looked at Upton, and he at me, as the song wound down. And I don't know what he was thinking, but in the end I could have hugged Mary for her choice of music.

Upton smiled at me. And I imagine he was thinking along the same lines as I about this place. And renewing his pledge to take care of it.

I wrote immediately, of course, to Miss Cunningham, telling her of the safe arrival of the harpsichord. I know that already the war has financially ruined her plantation in South Carolina. And that she is feeling physically more disabled every day. Yet she is determined, as if in a fight all her own, to restore to this place all the furnishings that belong here.

She wrote that the harpsichord came from Lorenzo Lewis, cousin of Mrs. Robert E. Lee. I know that Mary can write in fancy scrollwork, so I had her make out a little card and placed it on top of the harpsichord, telling how it came to be here. After all, we are part museum, aren't we?

Fifteen

In the glory that nature bestows upon us in these September days there has been another skirmish at Pohick Church. The weather was very damp yesterday evening, and the gunfire carried on the air. I have learned that General Washington was a vestryman there. Mrs. Frobel told me. She also came round to tell us that someone had taken the brass doorknobs from the church doors.

What is there in soldiers that is so dastardly? What makes them think they have a right to steal things away from where they fight? Does fighting bring out the worst elements in people? I saw Upton's brothers ride away, and though a Northerner, I was so proud of them. Would they steal after a skirmish? Does war turn all men bad?

The applesauce is finished. It will serve us all winter. We are now drying corn and putting away potatoes. Upton knows how to do all of this. I don't, but I am learning. He puts the potatoes in the root cellar, packed in hay. We are also drying some apples. Upton is harvesting sufficient wheat and a little rye. He also has vegetables in abundance. I am making blackberry preserves. I got Mary to go down to the river with me to pick some blackberries. She was entranced by the river and the fact that it has tides. She begged me to teach her to fish, and so I promised her I would.

I think she is bored here without many people coming and going who can admire her. One of the most important accomplishments she can imagine is to be admired.

We do have the soldiers visiting, though. Sometimes they come in bunches. Of course, it takes all our time to show them around, but then, they are paying twenty-five cents each. And another twenty-five if they want to see the general's bedroom, where he died.

There seems to be a rhythm about the place, like we move to the notes of a placid, old-fashioned tune, even though we are right between the lines.

Sometimes when I am outside and look into the woods, I fancy that I see soldiers on horseback riding through. They make no noise, however. They do not shout or fire guns, and even their horses' snorts are quiet. I wonder if I am seeing things. I wonder if it is the quiet of them that frightens me.

I asked Upton about it. "There is cavalry out there," he said. "They are the eyes of both armies. And they are always watching. Just mind your own business."

I forgot. Both his brothers are in the cavalry.

This week we had several hundred soldiers come to

visit, and they were very disorderly and trampled over everything. Upton had all he could do to manage them. And they all wanted a piece of brick or stone from the area of Washington's tomb. They actually chipped away at it. Upton had to scold them. They also wanted to take pieces of the branches of the holly trees along the garden walks.

So now Upton shows the soldiers the house and tomb and puts me in the sitting room, where from the windows I command a view of the garden walks and can chide them if they start taking holly.

Mary calls me stingy. "Let them have something to take away with them as a memento," she says. She is right. They want to take something from this place, but I cannot let them have the holly or pieces of the tomb. I must think of something that they can purchase when they leave.

Upton has solved the problem. The workmen have been making bricks here for purposes of restoration. Upton thinks we might put aside those he calculates we need and sell the rest as souvenirs. Many of the soldiers have money, and then at least they'll leave our holly alone. And it will help defray expenses.

I have a letter from Louisa Washington, John Augustine's oldest daughter, who is just sixteen. She assures me that her father's will is explicit and sound. And even though the family retains the rights to one quarter square acre around the general's tomb, none of his heirs will ever molest Mount Vernon.

What a lovely girl! I sent her a note, thanking her and saying we must meet as soon as is possible. What thoughtfulness. I feel ashamed, since I was not so thoughtful and considerate with her father.

We've had another visitor. The photographer Matthew Brady. He came in the west gate at sunset the other day, two mules pulling his "what is it?" wagon, which is what he calls the contrivance he drags around, in which he develops his pictures. He came with one of his assistants—or "field operatives," as he calls them—a man named Timothy O'Sullivan.

Upton put them up in the barn, cautioning Mr. Brady not to let any of his chemicals start a fire and burn the place down.

Here is a man who has seized the moment, and I admire him very much. He was at Fort Sumter to take pictures three days after the evacuation of the Union garrison. This will be a war of photographs, he says. His aim is to place these photographs in front of the people so they do not become complacent about the killing. He says he aims to photograph dead bodies. Well, I suppose he has a point. If people actually see what is being done, they won't be so eager to have parades and military celebrations in honor of the war.

We fed him and his assistant, and he showed us his equipment and asked to do photos of the house. Upton immediately struck a deal. He would pay if he could sell them. So Mr. Brady stayed two days photographing, and now we have some pictures of the house and the tomb to sell to soldiers.

Somehow I cannot adjust to photographs, however. They look so harsh, so real. They leave nothing to the imagination, but show every defect in place and person.

I know because Mary convinced Mr. Brady to photograph her, and she looked harsh and older than her years. I would not be photographed. I think Mary was disappointed. I much prefer Winslow Homer's sketch. But I think photography is both the blessing and the curse of the future.

I promised to teach Mary to fish, and so I did. The herring are running, of course. The neighbors call it "a rare delicacy and steady diet."

Upton was out on our small rowboat that same day, fishing for herring, which he salts down in barrels for the winter and puts in the storehouse.

Mary and I were on the wharf, which is now repaired. She was happily holding her pole when I leaned over and, of all things, fell into the water! Well, of course I can swim. My brothers taught me as a child. But the most terribly embarrassing thing happened then. Mary stood up and called to Upton, who was far enough downriver not to see us, just around a little bend. He came rowing over, and just as he did she took off her hoopskirt and blouse and, in her chemise and pantalets, *right in front of Upton,* jumped in to save me.

Well, I would not be saved and told her so. "Get out of the water," I told her savagely, "as soon as I do. I'll hand you your dress. How dare you, in front of Upton?"

"I'm saving you," she shouted, all the while splashing about with her mouth open so the nearest herring could pop in.

"I don't need saving, Mary, but I'm afraid you do." My own hoopskirt was billowing about me, making it near impossible for me to make progress, but all the same keeping me afloat, so I made it to the wharf like a great whale.

"We're all right," I yelled to Upton. "Stay back."

But he didn't. He was out of the boat before I could say another word, swimming toward me. He guided me to the wharf, got me up, then reached for Mary, who of course had her arms outstretched like a true damsel in distress.

Then he lifted her out. Her chemise and pantalets clung to her, dripping, and I was so ashamed for her that I reached for the shawl we'd been sitting on and wrapped it around her. "Get up to the house!" I scolded. "Mary, I'm responsible for you while you are here."

"I didn't drown, did I?"

"It isn't drowning I'm talking about."

I glanced back. Upton was swimming back to his small rowboat, not looking at us.

I am convinced that Mary did it purposely. And another thing I am convinced of now: All this while she has had an eye out for Upton. All this snapping at him, arguing with him, and sassing him has been her way of getting attention.

And what does he think of her? I find that it worries me.

Sixteen

I had to scold Mary. I had to play Miss Semple. And if I must say so myself, I did it with rather a firm hand and voice.

"How *could* you do such a thing as to take off your clothes in front of him?"

"Heavens, Sarah, I didn't know you could swim. I was saving you."

"You know my brothers taught me. We used to go swimming in the creek at home."

"Well, this was a *river. With tides.* I was thinking of you, Sarah."

"Well, thank you, but I have to say that I think you were thinking of yourself."

"Do you accuse me of showing my charms to Upton?"

"Yes, I do."

"Well, I am precious insulted, I can tell you."

We were quarreling upstairs. Away from the servants. Yet I knew every one of them was listening. The house itself had ears.

"I don't care how insulted you are, Mary. I don't care a fig for your feelings. What you don't know is how people around here gossip. And we can't afford gossip. This situation we have here is tenuous enough as it is."

"People!" She laughed. "What people? You don't consider the servants people, do you?"

"Yes, I do. I do consider them people, Mary. But besides them, there are eyes and ears all over this place. Tomorrow we're likely to read in the *Washington Star* that we were frolicking without our clothes on in the river with the superintendent. Don't you understand?" I appealed to her. I told her other charges that had been thrown at me. Even the business about being a spy. "We must keep the name of the Association spotless," I finished. "No scandal."

"Well, I thank you, but I have to say that I can't see what my honestly trying to save you from drowning has to do with all this," she said.

She would not see. I could not make her.

"Do you want me to leave?" she asked. "I'll leave this place if I cause so much trouble for you, Sarah."

I said no. I should have agreed and said yes.

"You know," she said, drying her hair with a towel, "you ought to ask yourself why you are really taking on so, Sarah. Is it because you are jealous?"

"Of what?" My heart lurched inside me.

"I mean, do you like Upton yourself? Do you favor him? Or are you too prissy to acknowledge it?"

It was as if she had slapped me. But I was never

tongue-tied. And I felt years older than her. She was acting no better than a schoolgirl.

"My feelings are my own," I said.

"You could at least admit them to me so I know."

"Know what?"

"If you harbor feelings for him. If there is an understanding between you. If there is, I will leave, Sarah. I will take myself out of the picture."

"There is no picture," I said.

We exchanged a long look. I could see she did not believe me, or was at least unsure. "Thank you, Sarah. Then, I shall stay," she said.

Upton came and apologized to me. "I only wanted to get her out of the water," he said.

"It's all right." I was shelling peas in the detached kitchen. Helping Jane get supper. I liked shelling peas, and Jane was teaching me about cooking.

"It isn't all right. I know what you're thinking." He paused to cough. It was deep and resounding.

"Are you ill?" I asked. "That dip in the water did you no good. It was cold."

"No, I'm fine, thank you. I just don't like seeing you upset. I know you worry about the propriety of things."

"Well, at least you understand," I said. "After all, Mary is a beautiful young girl, and if you are attracted, I don't blame you at all, but she is a bit of a coquette."

He looked at his shoes. A piece of his brown curly hair fell over his forehead. He wore his hair longish. "I'm not attracted," he said. "And I'm not altogether untried in dealing with such girls. The South is full of them."

"I never asked you if you had a . . ." I paused. "Anyone who interested you."

"I didn't ask you, either. I didn't think that's what we were about here."

"We aren't," I said abruptly.

He nodded his head as if something had been settled, when I knew nothing had. He made some excuse about seeing soldiers coming and left the kitchen.

Soldiers were coming. Several of them. Upton was seeing to them, however, so I went on shelling the peas. I didn't know where Mary was, and frankly I didn't care.

After about half an hour Upton came back into the kitchen. I was determined to make a pie for supper and was rolling out the dough.

"I'm afraid we have trouble, Sarah," he said.

I went with him. And yes, we did have trouble. He'd given the soldiers their tour of the tomb, then on the way to bringing them to the house found one of their members lying under a tree in a delirium of sickness.

I went with Upton to see him.

They were from the Fifth Michigan, six of them. The

one on the ground was called Pomeroy. "He has congestive fever, ma'am," a corporal told me.

"He should be in the hospital," I said. I'd leaned over him to find his head hot.

"He was released from the hospital," the corporal said, "and told to take his ease."

"Then, why is he here?"

"He wanted to come, ma'am."

Somehow his companions got him into the house. Upton and the young man's friends did what they could. They laid him down on the settee in the Little Parlor. They gave him water. They cooled his brow.

He was shaking and sweating all at the same time. Upton got him undressed, down to his skivvies, and covered him with a blanket.

We fed the soldiers. I went into the kitchen with Jane to help, and Mary came and sat beside the sick soldier.

What to do with him? "We've sent for an ambulance to take him back," the corporal said.

"He can't be moved," was my first reply.

"We don't want to impose on you."

I looked at Upton, but he did not return the look. He did not appear too chipper himself. He was coughing again. I became worried. There is a swampy bit of land a quarter of a mile below the mansion. Upton calls it "a marsh filled with pestilence." General Washington called it "the hell hole." It is guaranteed every year, in the hot season, to cause illness, being a breeding place for mosquitoes, and is responsible every year for a sickness of chills and fever. Had Upton contracted something from working near it?

"I don't care if you've sent for eight ambulances," I snapped. "You aren't moving him. He's staying here. Don't worry about the bother."

"I'll stay with him," the corporal said. "You all go back to camp and tell the captain."

It was agreed, and the corporal, whose name is Derwent Dwight, has taken up his post beside his friend's sickbed.

My pie crust burned in the oven. The peas were overcooked. Altogether it was not a good night. And upon retiring, Upton was coughing more than ever.

I heard him during the night. The cough resounded through the quiet house like a drum, scraping on my nerves. *I should make him some hot tea with honey in it*, I thought. So I got up, put on a robe, and went downstairs to the kitchen, where I lit an oil lamp and made the tea. I put a drop of bourbon in it to help him sleep, then went back upstairs.

Mary was there before me. She was kneeling at his bed. She had a bowl of water and a cloth, and she was wiping his brow, his face, and his chest where his nightshirt was open.

"Mary." My whisper was loud.

"Oh, hello, Sarah. I just thought I'd help. He's feverish."

"Go to bed."

"Why?" she asked innocently.

"Because he's delirious, too, and he wouldn't have you here like this if he weren't."

She wrung out the cloth. "Oh, and I suppose he'd have you?"

"It isn't my intention to wash him. I'm bringing him tea. If he needs washing, I'll get Priscilla. Or Dandridge."

She laughed, a lilting sound, and stood up. "At least I'm more honest than you, Sarah. At least I admit I'm fond of him. Who's to be ashamed here if the truth were known, anyway?"

"Go and get me Priscilla," I said sharply. "She sleeps above the kitchen now, since you're here. Tell her I need her."

Upton coughed again. I did need Priscilla. I couldn't hold up his head and hold the cup without spilling it. "Go!" I ordered.

She went, and Priscilla came back along. She knew what to do. In no time she had a remedy made and Upton's cough quieted, and she sent me to bed.

As I passed Mary's room I saw it was dark. *She'll sleep late in the morning,* I thought. I heard nothing from below-stairs, so I assumed the young soldier and his friend were all right. Priscilla set herself up in a chair next to Upton. I went to bed.

In the morning young Pomeroy was still very sick. Priscilla immediately made him a mustard footbath and other remedies. He slept most of the time. His captain and his ambulance came to inspect him. The captain was from Detroit, Michigan, and didn't seem to care a fig for General Washington's home or the fact that he stood in General Washington's Little Parlor. He was polite as could be, but all he wanted was Pomeroy returned to him.

"This damned South—excuse me, miss, but this damned climate isn't good for anybody. Needs some good Michigan air, is what he needs."

"I think we do all right, Captain," I told him.

He smiled at me. He was very handsome, with a beard and mustache. He'd ridden in on his own horse, alongside the ambulance.

"He's been calling for his wife," I said.

"He's married only one month."

"How terrible."

"We should have a doctor. I couldn't get one to come," he said.

"Priscilla is as good as a doctor."

"You say he can stay one more day?"

"I say he can stay as long as he likes, Captain, but if you wish to come back tomorrow, you may."

He sighed and looked around. "What kind of a place is

this? Your home? You one of those Southern belles I've heard about?"

"No, sir. I'm not one of those Southern belles you've heard about. I'm from Troy, New York. This is the home of General Washington." And I told him why I was here.

"Good girl. You're a good girl, you know that?" he said when he left. "God, I always said it. The women have all the brains in this outfit."

What "outfit" he was talking about, I didn't know. But he said he'd return tomorrow.

He left around eleven, I recollect. Around noontime I went up to wake Mary. Often she'd slept until noon, but seldom later. I knocked on her door. There was no answer. I opened it and went in.

Her bed was made, the quilt smoothed over carefully. A note was in the middle of it.

> *Dear Sarah:*
>
> *I have left. I saw my chance when the captain came by earlier today. I sneaked downstairs and out the side door and asked him for a ride back to Washington. He was most accommodating, even let me have time to write this note.*
>
> *I shall be in touch with you. I am sorry, but this hasn't turned out. I am attracted to Upton and cannot deny it. So are you, but you insist*

on denying it. All this means is trouble for
everybody. I am going back to Philadelphia.
I shall write.

> *Your friend,*
> *Mary McMakin*

I stood there holding the note to my breast. How had she done all this without my knowing? There was no second-guessing Mary. She was quicker than a rabbit in the celery patch. Me? I'm slow. I stood there like a jackass in the rain, blushing over the contents of her note. Then I ripped it up, lest someone find it.

Better she's gone, I told myself as I went about my duties that day. Her being here would mean nothing but trouble. We must keep everything spotlessly aboveboard for the Association or this whole experiment will fail. And then what will happen to George Washington's home, Miss Cunningham, who is counting on me so, and the Association?

Seventeen

I moved Priscilla back into my room. I missed Mary and I felt guilty about her. Not only had she left suddenly, she had left without saying good-bye, with only the ambulance captain for guidance. I had heard that there was a lot of sickness in Washington too, as well as the usual chaos. Would she be able to get her connections back to Philadelphia?

I felt responsible for her. Now I had two people to feel guilty about, Mary and John Augustine Washington. But I must think of the greater good, the possibility she posed of gossip against the Association. Oh, it is not always easy to do the right thing. But then, Miss Semple told us that, only I didn't understand her at the time.

"I am not good with people," I told Upton when he was up on his feet again after a week.

I did not tell him the real reason Mary left. When she was washing him, he'd been delirious. But I think he guessed that Mary and I had fought over him.

"She was a stubborn girl," was all he would say. "I'm sorry if any of it was my fault, Sarah."

"None of it was," I assured him. "I'll write to her and

make it right. She has been my friend since childhood."

Do men see things as women see them? Or do they just pretend certain things do not exist, to lessen the pain? I don't know. And like as not, I never will.

Private Pomeroy of the Fifth Michigan stayed four days, and then his captain and his ambulance came back to get him. I made it a point to see the captain when he came. We got to talking, and I told him how we were on a strict budget here, how we had lost money from visitors since the government took our boat and I must rack my brain to think of ways to bring in some cash. He suggested coffee beans. Yes, coffee beans! He told me that some people in the city are selling bracelets made from coffee beans and that soldiers are buying them. He said they sell this particular kind of bean at the Washington market.

Then he left us a generous donation. Ten whole dollars! That will go a long way toward buying food for this winter. And he said that Mary was fine, that he'd escorted her directly to the train station, where she managed to get a train for Philadelphia.

I wait for a letter from her. I cannot imagine what she will write to my sister, Fanny, and what blame she will put on me, but I am sure I shall hear from Fanny about the matter.

It is October 1. Upton reminded me this morning that there is no real border between the Confederacy and the

Union. That the only one that exists is at the foot of our sloping lawn. That seems to have put things back in perspective for me. Upton always seems to know the right thing to say when I am at sixes and sevens.

I am making a trip to the city to get some supplies. And I shall endeavor to get the coffee beans.

Oh, what a time. I haven't written in this journal in days because so much has happened. First, the wheel of my wagon broke in Alexandria on the way to the city. The wagon was full of cabbages and potatoes and apples to sell in the Washington market. The only other way to get to Washington was by the omnibus. So I hired a man in Alexandria to fix the wheel. He said he must keep the wagon overnight, that he could sell my vegetables for me in Alexandria and would have my money and my wagon waiting for us when we returned. So I had to trust him and leave my wagon, and take the omnibus with Priscilla. All went well in Washington. I managed to get the coffee beans I wanted, and we put them in two bags to even up the weight of them, and each carried one on the omnibus back to Alexandria.

But the omnibus was late and we had to wait. It was a beautiful day and I did not mind. But when it finally came, I realized we would not be back to Alexandria until dusk, which comes earlier now that it is October.

When we got to Alexandria, lo, there was my wagon with the horses and a small package in brown paper on the seat. I shook it and realized it was my money for the vegetables. But the man had left a note saying he could not wait and he hoped we had a safe journey home. Then, just as we were getting into the wagon, a lad of about fourteen came over.

"Uncle Andrew told me to drive you home," he said.

I told him it wasn't necessary.

"Uncle Andrew said it is," he insisted. "He said it isn't safe for two women alone. And that the sentries at the barricades are told not to let anyone through after five o'clock. That sometimes they shoot at intruders before asking for passes, once it gets dark."

A clock on the local bank said quarter past five.

"I'll get you through," the lad said. And he was straightforward and tall for his age and said he'd roamed these woods and roads all his life, so we said yes.

I let him drive. We passed the first sentry post without difficulty. The soldiers seemed to know the lad, and I had passes from McClellan for me and Priscilla. We were three more miles on the road when we came to another barricade. "I know another way," the boy said. His name was John. "These soldiers are hard ones. We'll find another road."

So we came back the three miles and took another road. After going a short distance, we met a large body of troops in the turn of the road where there had never been any before. Now, these were all Federal troops, but they were dusty and worn looking and appeared very mean. Instead of a sentinel, the officer came forward and said he was sorry, but we could go no farther this night. I showed him my pass, to no avail. He pointed in another direction and said that after going a short distance, I would find the road barricaded, but by crossing a field, we would find a road through the woods, which would eventually bring us to the right road.

"But you take a chance of being shot at," he said grimly.

I was determined to get home that night, however. We conferred and decided to chance it, even though it seemed as if we were literally going round Robin Hood's barn. Before quite reaching the barricade, we were stopped by more troops. The captain said it was impossible. But I would go on! I told him what the other officer had said. He did not believe there was such a road but asked for my pass. He read it and said again that he had not heard of such a road. A little sergeant standing by asked if he might go and see. The captain said yes.

We waited. Think of it! Waiting at night amidst soldiers and barricades, still six or eight miles from Mount Vernon. Oh, how I longed for home! Soon the sergeant came back and said there was a road, but a bad one. I said I would try it. The sergeant looked at me as if I were demented, shook his head, mumbled something about uppity women, and took down the bar so we could pass. Then he offered to act as a guide through the field. It was a pretty little road, narrow, and the trees lowered their branches to greet us as we passed.

We went on without any idea where the road would take us. Soon we found ourselves at the back entrance of a gentleman's farm. We passed through until we reached the house. I sent John in to inquire if we might pass through the farmer's road. The gentleman was very courtly and kind. He introduced himself as Mr. Cox and said he feared our troubles were not over, but if we could not get through, he and his wife would be happy to accommodate us for the night.

Another short drive. Another body of troops, an officer more decided than the rest. He could not let us by, even though I showed him my pass.

He said, "I could let you through with that pass, but some of my officers down the road are under orders to shoot anyone who approaches." I asked him to send a soldier with us. He did. And we passed the ones he said would shoot us without a word!

Then we turned to the road leading to Mount Vernon, and I felt safe. I said, "Drive fast, John, it's getting late!" And then another barricade, more formidable than the rest. The road was narrow and so situated that there seemed to be no outlet but straight ahead. And our horse was getting restless, for he was accustomed to the regular roads. There was a fence, however, and John went back to ask the lieutenant to allow one of his men to open it. He came himself, with five men, and said it could not be opened without cutting, which they were forbidden to do.

Oh, the army! Spare me from the army and its stupid rules! How they will ever win this war, I will never know. Then the men found a gate, farther down, opened it, and led the horse through. But they had to lift the wagon over the fence because it could not fit through. I knew where I was then. Once around this barricade, I could reach the blacksmith who shod horses at Mount Vernon, and I could leave the horse and wagon with him until morning.

One of the soldiers said I had better not attempt it with only a lad in attendance and a Nigra woman. He said there were more sentinels down the way that he could not be answerable for. The others said there was no chance of getting out that way, but that if I would stay at Mr. Cox's, they would help me the next day.

The gathering darkness was answer enough. So we backtracked all the way to the house of Mr. Cox. The lieutenant walked beside our wagon all the way back. He told us they had been cutting trees for four days to stop the Confederate cavalry from passing. I did not tell him what nonsense I thought the whole war was. I dared not, they were being so serious and so nice.

Mr. and Mrs. Cox welcomed us and gave us hot tea and excellent accommodations. They even had a place for young

John. But when I looked out the window of my room and saw the soldiers' arms glittering in the lantern light, I thought that if there was an attack, which they seemed to be expecting, it might be pleasanter to be somewhere else after all.

In the morning the captain came to say his men had found a way for me to get around. I sent John home, with thanks to him and his uncle, and with some coins in his pocket. And we commenced our winding way. We found another farm, where there were two soldiers willing to show us the way. We came into a road, and they said soon we would find the last barricade. This we reached in safety and found three soldiers, who took down a fence and led us through some bushes and briars, down a hill, over a ditch, and through another fence, and congratulated us on finally being on a clear road. And believe me, I was grateful!

All for coffee beans!

When we got home, of course, Upton acted like one of my older brothers, alternately scolding and expressing his joy that we were all right.

"I waited up all night for you," he said sternly. "I imagined all sorts of things happening. You could even have stayed in Washington, for all I knew. I can't go through a night like this again, Sarah."

I finally convinced him it was not my fault. I showed him the money I had made on the vegetables, and he vowed to find Uncle Andrew's last name and thank him for the offer of his nephew for a guide.

"That will be all the trips to Washington for a while," he said sternly.

I smiled. I think he cares about me a little bit. The thought warms me.

Eighteen

As October advances, the leaves have turned bright yellow, red, and brown. Everything outside is so beautiful I don't want to come inside. I keep inventing tasks to keep me outside. My crow still visits me every day, and I feed him bread crumbs. I must remember to feed him all winter. He hops around the brick fence around the garden and scolds me all the time.

There are bright red berries on the dogwood trees at the edges of the woods. And large scarlet berries on the holly hedge near the mansion. Mornings the mist rises off the river, and the mallard ducks are flying south, over the river, right past Mount Vernon. Upton and Dandridge are hunting together. Upton tells me that from November through January the canvasback ducks will be flying, and they are good for eating too. We shan't be hungry this winter. And Upton and Dandridge have seen to it that a goodly supply of wood is in. So we'll have many a warm night by the fire. And then the shad and herring begin to run in the Potomac in April.

Upton has found a way to bore holes in the coffee beans so I can string them together to make bracelets. We work on this in the evening by candlelight. I think of Mary and how she could be playing the harpsichord for us, but then, likely she'd be up to some trickery if she were here, to make me angry with her.

"Were you taken with her?" I had the nerve to ask Upton one evening.

He didn't answer right off. He is not the kind of man to be put to such a question. And at first I thought he was angry for the asking. But presently he answered. "No," he said. "She was pretty and a little flirt, and no man is above liking such tactics, just for a minute or so. What man wouldn't be attracted? But no, I'm taken with someone else."

My heart fell inside me, when I thought I had it secure against such feelings. He led me to believe it was someone off the plantation, someone his brother had introduced him to. He does go sometimes to his brother's place nearby here to look after things. I know his brother has a lot of female admirers. I also know that Upton has a young woman living with her older sister and her sister's husband at his place, Bleak House, to care for it in his absence. I wonder if it is the younger sister. Upton never leaves here except to go once a month to check on Bleak House.

The first coffee bean bracelet worked out fine. The first night I made only two, but I know I can learn to work faster, and then we'll be able to sell them, as souvenirs, to soldiers who come by.

~

Dandridge has told Upton about Wes Ford. He is an eighty-two-year-old colored man who was a favorite of the Washington descendants. One of them, Judge Bushrod Washington, the son of the general's brother John Augustine, gave him a considerable amount of land on Little Hunting Creek, where he owns a farm.

Upton and I rode over today to see him. He has four children, all grown: William, Jane, Daniel, and Julia. All know how to read and write, as does Wes. The farm is in good standing, and he has many other holdings. I am amazed at this, but Upton is not. He told me that the Washingtons, Bushrod and his wife, took Ford into the house when he was a child, and it is said he was educated with their own children.

"Many times Southern families grow fond of a certain child and treat him or her as their own," he said.

I do not understand this business of slavery. I know Upton does, although he owns no slaves himself. He says he grew up with colored people in attendance upon him.

We found that Wes is just old and sometimes has attacks of delirium tremens. But his mind is in good order. Although his four children are willing to care for him, he keeps telling them he wants to "go home."

Home is Mount Vernon for him. He was once overseer here. His son William was once gardener. Upton has found a whole new cache of information now for what the place once looked like, and I know he intends to make use of it. Wes remembers how the gardens were laid out, and Upton is very excited about this.

So we brought Wes Ford home. He remembered the little room off the kitchen where he used to roost when he lived here, and was delighted to find it still intact. "I'll just stay in there," he said, "if it's all right with you all. It's near the kitchen and it's warm, and it's near the food."

The servants Jane, Priscilla, and Emily came to stare at him. They are amazed at his knowledge.

"One more mouth to feed," I heard Jane mumble as she went up the stairs to bed. But the others didn't seem to mind at all.

I have another scolding letter from Fanny, deriding me because of the argument between me and Mary. "So you are alone again," she writes, "with that superintendent. Mary tells me how handsome and dashing he is, that his family ties are actually with Washington himself. Those Southern men are all rapscallions, Sarah. I cannot upset Mother and Father by telling them of your indiscretion. I have two choices, it seems: to write to Miss Cunningham and tell her you are still only eighteen, or to come down there myself and hire another girl to stay with you. I am leaning toward the latter. Expect me soon. Your loving sister."

"But she can't come," I told Upton. I did not show him the letter, for fear it would make him uncomfortable. "She will never get through the lines. Look at what I went through just coming back here from Washington one night."

"I will write and explain to her that it is impossible," he offered.

"Then she'll write to Miss Cunningham and tell her I am only eighteen!"

"Let her, Sarah. Miss Cunningham can't do without you now. It's impossible for her to travel up here. Look at the envelope that letter came in." It was lying on the table. "It looks as if it's been to Europe and back. Mail is a doubtful matter these days. I'm afraid you'll just have to decide. Do you want her here? Or would you rather have her send a letter to Miss Cunningham, which likely won't get through? There is no more mail between the North and the South."

"There is if you use a special messenger."

"Being a Northerner, away from the fighting, she won't know that. Just let her write, and bide your time."

What Upton said was right. He thinks so clearly. And he always manages to make me feel better. Oh, I am afraid I am having feelings for him. My sister's letter brings them to light. It makes me look inward, where I don't want to look.

Yes, I do have feelings for Upton. They have been sitting all along inside me, growing, like baby birds in a nest. Getting ready to fly.

I cannot let them fly. I must rein them in and act like a proper woman. Oh, what would Miss Semple have to say about all this? She always did say that when affairs come to a head between a man and a woman, it's usually the woman's doing. Constantly she reminded "her girls" of the responsibility they had of keeping things proper. Because men are so frail and vulnerable, she told us. They can be led around by the nose by us women. "And if ever one of my girls gets into trouble, I will know it is her fault," she would say, "and not the young man's. The responsibility to maintain good behavior rests with you, girls. Remember that."

Anyway, Upton has feelings for another. Didn't he tell me that?

Wes Ford is well ensconced in Mount Vernon again. Evenings by the fire he tells us stories. He tells how he was a carpenter here, a wheelwright and overseer of the house servants in Judge Bushrod's time.

He tells us how, in 1837, he and another man had to open the door of the tomb because there was a leak. "The general's mahogany coffin was nearly gone, the lid and the head part quite rotten," he said. "All we could see was the lead coffin. Before that, in 1832, I was there when the general's remains were inspected. The features, concealed in the winding sheet, were still in place. I myself put my hand over the winding sheet to determine that. But in 1837 the features had fallen in and the sheet was decayed."

He told us how he'd refused a bribe from a member of Congress to enter the house when John Augustine lived there. "He was good to me, John Augustine," he said. "Too bad he got killed in the war."

And he knows what the gardens once looked like, how the greenhouse should look if it is restored, and all the things Upton has been trying to find out. They spend many nights by the fire poring over plans.

Today Emily and Priscilla had a fight again. I came into the house after a walk, and they were near to scratching at each other in the kitchen.

After I pulled them apart, I demanded to know what the fight was about. "I's the oldest," Priscilla said. "I's supposed to take care of Wes Ford. I's supposed to give him his medicine from the doctor and make sure he eats. Not her."

"He likes me better, you old silly you." Emily was crying. Her face was swollen and red. It looked as if Priscilla had slapped her. I had to scold them both and come up with a remedy. They should take turns helping Wes Ford. One week for one, and one for the other.

Personally I agree with Emily. I think Priscilla is an old silly.

We are starting to restore Martha Washington's room. Wes tells us that Billy Lee told him that Martha used to have certain of the slaves into her room in a sewing circle. "They had to be mulatto, like my children are," he told us. "And those in the circle were the envy of all on the plantation."

It is good that Wes knew Billy Lee. In 1802, when Wes came here, Billy Lee was still alive. "Billy died in 1828," he told us, "and all those years I listened to his stories. He served with the master more than thirty years. All through the war he was by his side. He hunted with him and attended him faithfully."

As the fire crackled at night, and the autumn wind and leaves rattled around the house and we roasted chestnuts, Wes's creaky voice imparted to us the stories of how it was in the general's time, handed down from Billy Lee.

Both Upton and I know we have a treasure in Wes. It is as if another genuine piece from the house, like the harpsichord, has been returned to us.

Nineteen

One would think there was no war on. And there really hasn't been all this fall. Everyone is complaining because McClellan is letting the beautiful fall days slip by without using his army. On both sides, it seems, the generals and leaders meet and bicker, like Emily and Priscilla in the kitchen. The papers say they are discussing grand strategy. It sounds so much like men!

Oh, there have been skirmishes. One at Springfield Station here in Virginia, another in Missouri, of all places. I cannot imagine this war reaching all the way into Missouri. Upton says that he read that the citizens of Chincoteague Island, Accomac County, here in Virginia, all took the oath of allegiance to the United States before Federal naval officers.

The country truly is torn apart.

In the middle of the month there was a battle. Some call it Ball's Bluff, others the Battle of Leesburg, here in Virginia. The Confederates won.

It frightens me. Suppose they win the war? What kind of country will this be? Two countries, I suppose. And Upton will live in one and I in the other.

~

There is more news. We have nothing confirmed yet, but some soldiers who visited told us that the western part of Virginia has broken off from the rest of the state and gone Union. My word, those people took a stand! And here I sit, struggling to remain neutral, making the soldiers put shawls over their uniforms before they visit the tomb!

Here I sit, making coffee bean bracelets. Will I be sorry for all this someday? I wish I could really do something for the war. Now I know how Upton feels, having to stay out of the army.

Today I got so excited. A messenger delivered a letter from Mary in Philadelphia. I was excited because I'd written to her apologizing for my part of the fracas, and now I would know she had forgiven me.

But it was not to be. And my spirits not only fell, they crashed to the very floor of my soul and broke to pieces inside me.

What she said I could scarce believe.

She said my family had arranged all of it, all of this for me. From the very beginning.

"You think you went against your mother and father when you took the job?" she asked. "They planned the whole thing because they had been told about Upton Herbert, and they saw him as a good husband for you. Of course, the idea was mentioned casually in front of you by your mother and father's friends, and you jumped at it. You had the Maxwells and Goodriches write letters for an interview, yes. Well, whose friends are they? Your parents'. Your mother and father allowed you to think the idea was yours and even objected somewhat, if you will recall.

"No, age was never mentioned by anybody. But I know that after you wrote to Miss Cunningham, your mother and father wrote, asking if you could have the job. She was urged to keep it secret from you. I know you lied about your age, because Upton told me you had. Only to ask me to keep it a secret.

"You think you are so smart, Sarah Tracy. Which is why I was so angry. I knew about the whole thing. Your family kept writing and asking me to come to you there and act as chaperone. You see, the whole thing was arranged with my collusion, because I was supposed to be chaperone. Then my mother became sick, and I couldn't come. Then other things happened. I broke my ankle. I was afraid.

"They kept writing to me, asking me to come. Reminding me of my obligation. So I came. And look what happened. Tell me, do you think I would have flirted seriously with Upton when I knew this had been arranged for your benefit? I was just being helpful. Which is why I am so hurt. And I shall not forgive you."

Oh! The deceit of it! Oh, I walked around all day bumping into things because I could not believe it. I was so angry with my family! So humiliated. It all had been arranged.

And my parents had helped! And Miss Cunningham knew of it but never said.

I felt so humiliated! My mind whirled, trying to put it all together. So, they had planned this all, sent me here, let me walk into all of this.

They had made me think it was my idea! Allowed me to think I was deceiving them, rebelling against them.

I felt like a fly walking into the trap of a spider. Oh, I'd felt so superior, so smart. And it was just one more place they'd arranged for me to go, like New York City or Maryland, to find a husband!

I was a horse again, being sent to the auctions in Kentucky!

All day my mind kept going round and round, trying to put the whole thing together, trying to figure out who'd had a part in the deceit and who hadn't. And then my mind stopped.

Did Upton know?

Oh, I couldn't bear it if he knew! I'd die!

I'd leave tomorrow if he knew. I couldn't stay. I racked my brain trying to remember things he'd said to me, ways he'd acted, to determine if he knew. But I could find none.

So, what to do then? Go on as if nothing had happened? Fool them all? Or confront Upton and decide then and there?

Oh, I must think about it. I must give myself time. That was it. I'd take Miss Semple's advice. "Girls, if you are ever in a quandary, don't make instant decisions unless your life depends upon it. Think it over a day. Sleep on it."

I would do that. I would sleep on it.

Oh, that terrible Mary! I'd write and give her a piece of my mind. I would.

But then something else happened to make me forget my troubles.

A letter came by special messenger from Mrs. Burke, wife of the man who owns the bank in Alexandria with Upton's brother Arthur.

It was addressed to me.

Upton handed it to me, scowling, for at first he had thought it was bad news about Colonel Arthur Herbert, his brother. But then, why would it be addressed to me?

"Do you know her very well?" he asked.

"No." I opened the letter.

"Mrs. Burke wants me to come to their house tomorrow," I said. "And bring a basket of fresh eggs."

More scowling. "Something is wrong," Upton said. "They buy their eggs in Alexandria."

"She wants me to come alone."

"Something's not right," Upton insisted.

"Well, I'm going anyway," I said with firmness. I wasn't going to let him boss me around, even though he was picked for me as a husband. I felt a surge of excitement. Maybe I would finally be asked to do something for the war.

Martha Burke was, after all, the great-granddaughter of Thomas Jefferson. She had been born at Monticello. I busied myself the rest of the day, all the while thinking wild thoughts. I imagined her the center of a spy ring, and me helping her. But the spy ring would be Southern, then, wouldn't it? No, I convinced myself, it would be Northern. Because of her heritage she would want to save the country. I had heard of Southerners all over who were secretly with the Union.

And if it was Southern, why, I could politely refuse to help, saying I must stay neutral.

But here is my chance to do something.

Well, I was right. At least partway. And I have done something important! Oh, it was so exciting!

Early in the morning I set out down the long road from Mount Vernon to Alexandria. Alone. And with a basket of fresh eggs in the buggy.

I first passed Gum Springs, where the colored descendants of Washington's slaves live. Then another five miles, through camps of soldiers who all looked and waved. Some shouted. Some whistled. Some tipped their hats as I went by. I kept my head high and looked straight ahead.

I'd taken this road many times. I was not afraid. When I got to Alexandria, I saw that the little town was filled to the brim with soldiers. They loitered on the brick walks. They walked in groups. They were going in and out of the stores. And there seemed to be an inordinate amount of civilians, too.

Finally I got to John and Martha's house and went inside.

It was like a social visit. Martha had her maid serve me tea and biscuits. She asked about Mount Vernon and Upton. I told her how we'd brought Wes Ford to live with us and the stories he knew about General Washington.

All the while my basket of eggs rested on the floor. She did not ask for them.

Then Mr. Burke came in, bade me hello, sat down, and spoke quietly to me.

"Miss Tracy," he said, "I wonder if you could help us and do something for the Washington family."

"John Augustine's?"

"Yes."

"Of course," I said.

So he told me what he wanted. It seems that when the Union army took Alexandria, the money and bonds that the Association had paid John Augustine for Mount Vernon were in a safe in the Burke and Herbert Bank.

Then, the other day, came an order from the Union headquarters that the money was to be confiscated. So Mr. Burke took the money and bonds from the bank safe and brought them home. There he hid them in the mahogany wardrobe in their bedroom.

Union soldiers had come two days ago, asking for the

money. They searched the house from bottom to top, going into every crevice, upsetting clothes, dishes, books, personal papers. But they did not look in the mahogany wardrobe.

"But I knew they soon would," he said. "Because they said they would be back. So yesterday I got an old friend who is a carpenter to come to the house. He lifted a board in the hallway upstairs and put the money underneath. But we knew the search party was coming back. Today. So that's why we wrote to you."

"What do you want me to do?" I asked. Though I already knew. Though my heart was beating rapidly.

"I want you to empty the eggs out of your basket," he said. "I will pull up the floorboard and get out the money and bonds. I will put them in the bottom of your basket, then I'll put the eggs on top. Then, if you would be so kind, Miss Tracy, you could ride into Washington City. Go to Mr. Riggs's bank and there rent a safety-deposit box. And put the money in and bring me back the key. Do you think you can do that for us? And for the Washington family? And the Association?"

Yes, I thought I could. Yes, I would. I did, after all, have things to make up for with John Augustine Washington.

I bade them good-bye. Then, like the perfect little woman of the house, I got into my buggy with the basket. I set it down carefully so the eggs would not be broken, turned the horse's head, waved good-bye so all within sight, who were mostly soldiers, could see me, and drove ahead on the road to Washington.

I must have passed tens of thousands of soldiers, both walking in groups and in camps. Again some waved and some gave impertinent catcalls and some raised their hats. And I played the demure farm girl delivering eggs.

At every sentry point, of course, I was stopped. I had to show my pass. I was, at two stops, asked about the eggs.

"Who are they for?" one sentry asked me.

"Friends in Washington." I must continue to look pleasant. I mustn't be frightened.

"You wouldn't care to sell some to us?"

That was their concern. They wanted fresh eggs. "No, I'm afraid I must bring these to my friend. She's sickly, and the ones in Washington aren't that fresh off the farm."

"The only thing fresh off the farm in Washington is our president," one of the men said. And I saw his officer scowl. But they let me pass.

Each time I had to stop, my heart raced. I felt my hands sweat. But I flashed my most flirtatious smile, which I hated to do, and always said something nice to the soldiers, and soon they were distracted enough not even to see the basket of eggs.

I crossed the bridge without difficulty too and got into the city. The sun had disappeared behind the clouds, and the day was getting chilled. But oh, the city seemed so different from the last time I was there. Rather than marching, soldiers seemed to slink about and not look at anybody. There were no waving flags, no martial music, no young girls gathered around the encampments.

And in the chilled autumn, regiments were still encamped in tents on the hills. The smell of things burned lingered in the air. There were broken bales of hay in the streets. And I saw three or four dead horses.

I went straight to the Riggs bank and tied my horse in front. I brought my basket of eggs with me. Mr. Riggs was waiting.

He came over to me and took my hand, and showed me where to set the basket down. He picked up an egg, held it to the light, sniffed it, and exclaimed how fresh it seemed. Then he took the basket into the back room and I waited.

A clerk smiled at me. "Isn't it a shame about the fire," he said.

He told me then what had happened and why the city smelled. Near the observatory, in the corrals, thousands of horses were stabled for the army. One evening the stables caught fire, and it began to spread. Hundreds of soldiers and citizens alike volunteered to cut loose the horses. Once loosed, the poor animals ran through the dark, to the common along Rock Creek, and into Washington's streets. Wild and frightened, they galloped down Massachusetts Avenue. Some ran over the canal bridges into the Seventh Ward. Some ended up in gullies. Two hundred died in the stables.

"War," I said. "It kills not only those on the battlefield."
And I felt sad for the horses and angry for the stupidity of
those who were supposed to care for them.

"Is that why everyone seems so cast down in the city?" I
asked the clerk.

"No," he said. "They are cast down because of recent battle
losses. Because there are no orders to go into winter quarters."

We talked awhile longer. I wanted to appear like an
ordinary citizen just waiting for her payment for the eggs.

Then Mr. Riggs came back, handed me my basket and
my money for the eggs, and walked me outside. There he
gave me the key to the safety-deposit box to give to Mr.
Burke.

"You have done a wonderful thing," he said. "You have
saved the money and bonds for John Augustine's children.
Between what you are doing to save Mount Vernon and
what you did with this money, Miss Tracy, the Washington
family owes you much."

"They owe me nothing," I told him. But there was a
warm feeling of peace inside me, a feeling of rightness,
finally, about what I was doing.

I decided, on the ride home, that even if Upton Herbert
knew what my family had done, arranging for me to come to
Mount Vernon because of him, I would not leave. Mayhap
this has been all their idea, but it has become my life. I have
made a promise to people, indeed to the Washingtons,
coming here.

My parents could not begin to know the wherefores and whys of it. They are mine alone, to keep and nurture. I'll be here in the spring to plant the gardens, to sweep the winter out of the corners of the grand old house.

I'll be here as long as Miss Cunningham needs me.

Now all I need to do is make things right with Upton.

Twenty

I must write the rest of it before I go to bed this night, though the hour is late. I cannot sleep, for I must capture my feelings before the morning light seeks them out and renders them weak and without meaning.

I did not intend to confront Upton immediately. I intended to go about my business quietly and efficiently. I delivered the key back to Mr. and Mrs. Burke, and by the time I returned home it was near eight at night.

It was dark when I drove the buggy into the west gate. In back of the house Upton was waiting for me. Once again he was angry.

First he asked if I was all right. When I said I was, he inquired about the nature of my day. And when I told him, he exploded.

"Money and bonds into Washington?" he repeated. "Are you daft, Sarah?"

"I suppose so. In many ways."

Dandridge came to take the horse and buggy. And while he was with us, Upton said nothing. But he paced in the dark. Priscilla was waiting in the shadows of the doorway.

"They've kept supper for you," Upton said finally when Dandridge had left.

"Good." I started to make for the back door, but he stayed me with a hand on my arm.

"You can't do these things, Sarah. I worry. I feel as if I am responsible for you."

I looked at him and he at me. And I knew then that he knew of the arrangement, that he'd known all along. And more than that I saw something in his eyes that I'd seen before but never recognized.

I saw that he wished to speak of it.

The knowing sat heavy on him. And he wanted to share it with me. But he didn't know how.

I told him he was not responsible for me. I told him I was my own person.

"I worry about you, chasing all about as you do. How do you think I feel? I can't even go into Alexandria anymore. And it was once my hometown."

I told him I was sorry. He nodded solemnly, wanting to say more. I waited.

"I am troubled by things I cannot speak of, Sarah," he said then. "I have come to hold you in great esteem, and I would speak to you of them."

The lingering touch of Southern accent, the way he stood there in the dark, which was relieved only by the burning torches he'd set in their holders this side of the bowling green, the thrust of his strong chin, the way he held his head, all made me say what I never meant to say.

"Tell me of them."

"It's late," he said. "You are tired."

But I persisted. "Is it about what was in the letter I received from Mary the other day?" I asked him.

He said he did not know the contents of the letter. But I suspect he did, for I think mayhap Mary had told him of the arrangement.

"I think you do," I said. "Leastways, I think you know what Mary was keeping from me until that letter."

He nodded yes. That is all. He just nodded yes. Slowly.

My heart leaped and expanded in my chest. *Oh, Upton,* I thought. And I said aloud, "So, all this time you knew."

He said yes. All this time he knew.

I apologized for my family. "They treat me as a horse," I said. "A prize horse they are auctioning off. They send me around as if to auctions, to the highest bidder."

"You are a prize," he said. "But don't think of yourself as a horse, or someone to be auctioned. All families do this with young women. In the South, too."

"I'm sorry they involved you," I told him. "I am embarrassed about it. I hope you don't feel . . ." I paused, seeking the right word. "Obligated in any way."

He told me not to be sorry. Or embarrassed. He said he was obligated. And then he paused. "I'm honored to be considered," he said.

"Well, I suppose a Southern gentleman would say such a thing," I told him with a little laugh. "It's too bad you are spoken for, Upton." I felt safe saying it. I felt sophisticated. After all, he was spoken for, wasn't he?

"I'm not spoken for," he said.

I felt hit in the face with cold water. My embarrassment went from my head to my toes. "But you said there was someone you cared for."

"There is," he told me.

"Oh." I said I supposed she was the younger sister of the people caring for his house. Or someone like that.

"She is someone like that," he said. "She is caring for a house. The trouble is, she is blind."

I wished there were a fence post to hold on to. I wished I were a fence post. Was he saying what I thought he was saying?

He was. And he did. It was the next thing he said, as a matter of fact. And no, I shan't write it here. Mayhap this is a journal, but who knows, my daughter might read it someday. Upton's and my daughter.

I will say, for my children's sake, that he did take me in his arms then. And that the darkness became light.

Then he said that we must be careful. And we must talk about what we would do next. And I agreed. Oh yes, I agreed.

We decided we will go along as we have been. I will not leave. I cannot leave, even though it might be the proper thing to do, given the circumstances between us.

We decided not to tell anyone. We decided to act, every moment we are together, as proper as we can, so as not to bring down any shame on what we are doing here. Or on the Association.

Oh, we might have touched hands when no one was looking. Or stolen a kiss in a dark corner. But no more. Ever. Not until all this is over. The war, everything.

After all, the first thing we must do is honor our responsibilities. People are depending on us.

As I know Upton, he cannot act with anything less than honor. It is part of why I love him, I think.

It will be difficult for us. We both agreed on that. But look at the sacrifices and the difficulties others are experiencing because of this dreadful war.

I think, after all, that I have finally found my part in it.

Epilogue

All through the long and dismal war Sarah and Upton continued to do their jobs, retained their dignity and honor, and never brought a word of criticism to the Association by their actions. And they were closely watched by those who would disrupt their goals.

They scrambled for food, welcomed soldiers, acted as host and hostess, received visitors, and made and sold coffee bean bracelets, bricks, and flowers to keep the place going. Sarah wrote to Miss Cunningham that the visiting soldiers were "crazy for flowers."

The Mount Vernon boat ran again in spring of 1862. General McClellan was relieved of his command and replaced by General Ambrose Burnside, who moved his troops south through the Mount Vernon area in December of 1862 to attack General Lee. But the South won this battle, and the Union army retreated north, and Sarah and Upton and others at Mount Vernon could hear their sad passage as they returned with wounded in the wagons and defeat on their faces.

General Burnside was replaced by General Joseph Hooker, and in the spring of 1863 the Union army suffered a severe defeat at Chancellorsville, forty miles from Mount Vernon. General Hooker was replaced by General George Meade. Southern general Stonewall Jackson was killed. And the carnage went on.

At Mount Vernon, Sarah Tracy and Upton Herbert continued to keep the place safe, but every time a Northern commander was replaced with a new one, Sarah had to appeal to the new commander for a promise that Mount Vernon would remain a sacred and neutral ground, the only neutral ground in the country during the sad and destructive war.

All around the Mount Vernon area, property, fences, and crops were destroyed by the war. Horses were stolen in the night, and the Quakers especially suffered from such depredations.

In a letter to Miss Cunningham, Sarah wrote: "You have had no army twice and thrice through your place, every stalk of grain and hay, and every barn burned. Every hog, sheep and cow killed. Every pound of wheat and corn taken away and every horse. Every carriage carried off, and when they could not be, the wheels taken off and burned. I have heard nothing else for three years. But all we see who have lost everything and have to begin life anew, are cheerful and go to work like men and women. They have tried, and do try, to put aside the past and look only to the future. Alas, it is very hard for some."

She was speaking of her neighbors. Mount Vernon remained intact.

In 1865 the war ended, with the North victorious. Then came the long walk home for many soldiers, and those who could stopped at Mount Vernon to visit, to see General Washington's home and reaffirm their faith in their country and themselves.

Sarah continued to write to Miss Cunningham, making her daily reports. She made more than eight hundred bouquets of flowers to sell to soldiers to raise money, enough to put a new zinc roof on the tomb. She wrote, "The plants and flower seeds I bought with my own money."

Sarah Tracy left Mount Vernon in 1867. Her work was over there.

Upton Herbert continued as superintendent for one more year.

In 1872 Upton Herbert and Sarah Tracy were married in Philadelphia. No one knows why they waited so long after the war. There is much about this story that is not known, as with all stories. They made their home, for fourteen years, at Mr. Herbert's Bleak House, which was five miles from the Fairfax courthouse.

In 1886 the Mount Vernon Ladies' Association acquired a real appreciation of what had happened at Mount Vernon during the war years and how Sarah Tracy and Upton Herbert had played out a real life story there. They wrote to Sarah Herbert and asked if she would send to them any written account she had of those years. Sarah wrote back that their house had burned the Friday before Christmas in 1885, and they were living with Colonel Arthur Herbert, Upton's brother, near Alexandria.

She wrote that although silver, some private papers, clothing, and furniture were saved, the trunk on the second floor, in which were her papers from her years at Mount Vernon, had burned. How strange to think that throughout all those years she spent at Mount Vernon, in the middle of a terrible war, it remained safe, yet in peacetime it was lost when their own house burned!

All that remained were the letters she had written to Miss Cunningham.

Sarah Tracy and Upton Herbert are buried in Ivy Cemetery, in Fairfax County, Virginia. They had no children.

The Mount Vernon Ladies' Association still exists and runs General Washington's home today.

Author's Note

*T*his novel is *based* on the story of Sarah Tracy at Mount Vernon. For the sake of story I have moved some characters around, changed the chronology of some of the events that happened to them, and given them motivations, thoughts, and emotions that research does not provide.

But all the major happenings in the book really occurred. I made up none of them, except for the fight between Sarah and Mary. This was for the sake of story.

Sarah Tracy did write daily to Miss Cunningham. Her letters are preserved in the book *Mount Vernon: The Civil War Years* by Dorothy Troth Muir. This is one of the many books I used for research.

All the others I used as an updraft and flew with them on my own.

I am grateful to the writers of all the books I mention in my bibliography for providing the research I needed. But as a writer of fiction, I gave Sarah and Upton and the others a life they did not have in research. This is the job of a fiction writer, to create a satisfying story. And this story—of Sarah Tracy at a falling-down Mount Vernon, working with Upton Herbert not only to repair it, but to keep it from ruin and make it the only neutral ground in America during the Civil War—haunted me until I actually wrote it.

Bibliography

Blair, William. *Virginia's Private War: Feeding Body and Soul in the Confederacy, 1861–1865.* New York: Oxford University Press, 1998.

Boyce, Burke. *Man from Mount Vernon.* New York: Harper and Brothers, 1991.

Dalzell, Robert F., Jr., and Lee Baldwin Dalzell. *George Washington's Mount Vernon: At Home in Revolutionary America.* New York: Oxford University Press, 1998.

Greene, Constance McLaughlin. *Washington: A History of the Capital, 1800–1950.* Princeton: Princeton University Press, 1962.

Johnson, Gerald W. *Mount Vernon: The Story of a Shrine.* New York: Random House, 1953.

Leech, Margaret. *Reveille in Washinton, 1860–1865.* New York: Grosset & Dunlap, 1941.

Muir, Dorothy Troth. *Mount Vernon: The Civil War Years*. Mount Vernon, Virginia: The Mount Vernon Ladies' Association, 1993.

From 2-time Newbery Medalist
E. L. Konigsburg

Silent to the Bone
0-689-83602-3

*From the Mixed-up Files of
Mrs. Basil E. Frankweiler*
NEWBERY MEDAL WINNER
0-689-71181-6

The View from Saturday
NEWBERY MEDAL WINNER
0-689-81721-5

*Jennifer, Hecate, Macbeth,
William McKinley, and Me, Elizabeth*
NEWBERY HONOR BOOK
0-689-84625-8

Altogether, One at a Time
0-689-71290-1

The Dragon in the Ghetto Caper
0-689-82328-2

Father's Arcane Daughter
0-689-82680-X

Journey to an 800 Number
0-689-82679-6

*A Proud Taste for Scarlet
and Miniver*
0-689-84624-X

The Second Mrs. Gioconda
0-689-82121-2

Throwing Shadows
0-689-82120-4

Aladdin Paperbacks • Simon & Schuster Children's Publishing
www.SimonSaysKids.com